LATE NIGHT LICK VOLUME 5 PRESENTS CHRONICLES OF A BBW

A NOVEL BY

N. TROUBLE

Nene Capri Presents Publishing, LLC
PO Box 743432
Riverdale, GA 30274
770-515-9164
nenecapripresents@gmail.com

Late Night Lick: Chronicles of A BBW is a work of fiction. Names, characters, places, and incidents either are products of the author's imagination or are used fictitiously, and any resemblance to actual persons, living or dead, business establishments, events, or locales are entirely coincidental.

Cover Design: by Lashonda Johnson & Nene Capri
NeneCapri@gmail.com
& Ghostwriterinc2016@gmail.com

Book Interior Design by Ghostwriter Inc. Contact Us
Ghostwriterinc2016@gmail.com

CHRONICLES OF A BBW

CHAPTER ONE

Wilmington N.C.

"Damn, I love the way that big phat ass claps as you slam up and down on this dick."

"You love all this? This ain't too much woman for you, Big Daddy?"

"Nah, not at all. Stop talking so much and twerk that ass on this dick."

'Thap…thap…thap…'

"Oh, yes, like this! Give me that dick! Yeah, you, want this pussy?"

'Smack…'

Lady Plus smacked her ass with both hands, then spread her cheeks giving Antwan an up close and personal look of her swollen clit.

Antwan was ecstatic, the warm surge shooting from his sack to the base of his dick caused him to slow down his stroke and squeeze his long, thick cock. The sight of Lady Plus's ass moving in and out and smashing together sounded like a mini thunderstorm. He became aroused beyond all capability. Her huge 44' Triple D torpedos swung violently with each motion.

She peeped him salivating over her voluptuous breasts and teasingly cuffed one in her small, tiny hands. She rotated her wide 64' inch hip, while cautiously making sure her breasts didn't spill. She licked her coffee brown nipple. Antwan's mouth opened wide, jealousy seeped in his mind, as he wished it was his soft lips devouring those balloons especially made for him.

"Umm…it tastes good, too!" She teased, looking back at him.

He's still stunned at how wide her hips and ass spread, as she bent over the pink and white bed set. Her pink, white, and bright orange lace one-piece gave the scenery a tropical feel. Her long, jet-black hair curled up and began to stick against her beautiful, soft, puffy cheeks from sweat.

"Cum in this juicy, swollen pussy, Daddy Long Stroke! You know I love to feel that warm cum sliding up my guts," Lady Plus continued to make her ass twerk. Each motion became harder, faster and more intense.

"Yeah, Big Mama…take all this dick. What's my name?"

"Oh…oh…oh, yesss, right there. Right there, Daddy Long Stroke. Dadddyyy…Longgg…Strokeee!"

"Oh, shit," Antwan fumbled with his pants.

He quickly placed his rock-hard dick into his pants and clicked a button on his computer. The sound of a juggling lock could only mean one thing.

Kim barged into his office with suspicion written all over her face. "What you doing in here with the door locked and the lights so dim?"

"Good, afternoon to you too, my lovely wife."

"Hubby, why is it sooo…hot in here? Turn down the thermostat. Why do you insist on working under these conditions? Brighten the lights, I can barely see you." Kim turned the thermostat down, opened his office window and brightened the light ultimately completing her own demands

Hassana rushed in, "Mr. Mitchell…I'm so…I mean, I apologize for not notifying you, your wife was coming. I was in the bathroom."

"It's alright, Hassana, whether you buzzed in or not. My lovely wife would have still barged right in like she owns the place. Right Doll?" Antwan winked at Kim.

"Is that a problem? I just came to bring you lunch, before I head to the gym." Kim said, with a smirk.

"No, it's never a problem, Doll. I'm always delighted to be blessed with your beautiful presence." Now Antwan was smiling.

"Alright, then, I see where this is headed. Nice to see you again Mrs. Mitchell. Mr. Mitchell, I'll be at my desk if you need me." Hassana exited the office purposely leaving the door open.

"Well back to the hearty lunch I delivered. You got a fresh salad, organic carrot juice with a splash of cinnamon, and sliced pineapples. Got to keep my man fine and healthy." Kim placed two tuba wear containers on his cluttered desk.

"Yeah…cinnamon carrot juice, my favorite!"

"You don't have to be so sarcastic. I know you're not thrilled about us going vegan, but the doctors said it's healthy. We have to change our old ways, by eating right, getting proper exercise and lowering stress."

"Yeah, well the doctor also said sex is the best exercise and stress reliever." He clawed at her phat pussy, poking out of her tights.

"Stop…what are you doing? What's gotten into you lately? Last night you tried to get me to go down on you, and it's not even your birthday."

The blood in his dick was just beginning to settle. He was on the verge of coming before she busted in. Now he'd settle for her petite frame bent over his desk, as he pounded her from the back.

"Oh, excuse me, I forget *my wife* will only please me orally on my birthday and sometimes on our Anniversary."

"You're really trying to hurt my feelings lately. I'm sorry, I'm not some cum gurgling, dick sucking, freak mouth whore. You knew what type of woman I was when you married me. Now I'm super sexy and in shape, that should be more than enough to turn you on. I'm no longer 260 something pounds." Kim struck a pose.

She stood a tad bit taller than 5'6, her breasts were 32-B cups, her waist was tiny, and she had 32' inch hips. Most men would drool over her beauty. Especially once you included her red bone skin, red hair, brown freckles, and hazel brown eyes. It's wasn't that Antwan didn't love his wife or that he didn't still find her gorgeous. He just missed her curves, her thunder thighs, her huge breasts and the warm, cushiony feeling of melting in her skin, when she used to wrap those big thighs and strong arms around him, as he pounded away at her guts, not worried if he was hurting her old plus size frame. His dick thumped, trying to bust out his pants after thinking about the good ole days.

"Look, you're the one who had the problem with your weight. I loved you then, and I love you, now. What's the matter with a man wanting to feel the inside of his wife? A quickie at work used to be our thing before we got married. Now everything is traditional."

"*Traditional...traditional?* You know what, never mind, I'm going to let that go. We'll revisit this again, tonight. The door is wide open, so I know your secretary probably heard every word, by the way." Kim moved closer and whispered, "When are you going to get her to join you at the gym? She's a shrimp burger away from type two."

"That's very childish. Also, I must enlighten you on how those words make you unattractive. To sit here and degrade another strong, smart, black woman because of her weight is beyond low. Did they cut off part of your heart and brain, when you had that surgery? The woman I married, was beautiful inside and out. All two hundred and sixty something pounds of her." he scolded.

"You're right, I apologize. I don't know what came over me. Let me close the door. We can have that quickie you wanted." She looked at her watch. "I have ten minutes before my appointment."

"Nah, I'm good."

"What do you mean?" She rushed over and threw herself in his lap. "Come on, hubby, I don't want to leave, knowing you're still upset with me. I love you, Antwan." Kim smothered his soft lips with wet kisses.

"I love you, too, Kim! Yet, I'll have to decline the offer. Unfortunately, we spent too much time bickering. My client should be arriving any minute. Remember I told you about my plan to expand my company.

"Yes. You're talking about being a personal accountant for those young men at the *Tru Colors Brewing Company*?

"Yeah, I see you were listening, with minority and females rapidly joining the Brewing business which was once owned, operated, and ran by white men. I feel it's only right, I make my father proud, being that he was the first Black Accountant to open his own firm in, Wilmington, North Carolina."

"That's great Hubby. I'm sure Pops will be smiling in heaven. You've already done a wonderful job keeping the family business successful." Kim gave him another kiss.

This time it was passionate "I really do apologize for my behavior. Would you believe me if I told you I was jealous?"

"Jealous…jealous of who? Doll you have no reason at all to be jealous. You're the love of my life. The only woman I've loved since Elementary."

Kim turned to mush hearing Antwan declare his love for her. The bulge in his pants gave her all the reassurance she needed.

"I love you, too, hubby." She jumped up and headed for the door.

"Hate to see you leave but love to watch you walk away."

Kim turned around blushing from ear to ear. "That might get you something less traditional tonight."

Antwan shook his head and tried to figure out the beginning and ending to all the papers on his desk.

****

Twenty Minutes Later…

Sweat slid down his forehead, papers were scattered across his desk. His plush, yet compact, small office told many historical stories. From the chair passed down from his great-grandfather, who handmade it for his son, which was his grandfather, who passed it down to his father, who passed it down to him. Even the old school calculator Antwan crunched numbers on, was a graduation gift to his father from his grandmother. Feeling frustrated he began to chew on the tip of his pencil, a habit he'd gotten from his father.

Knock…knock…knock…

"Come in."

Hassana entered sporting a yellow blazer and a huge designer bag, that had to have costed two months' salary. Her chocolate skin glistened in the lights.

"Mr. Mitchell, I'm heading to lunch. You want me to pick you up something from Bojangles?"

"Yeah, get me some chicken and whatever sides you're having. By the way, can you help me out before you leave? I'm having a problem acquiring and carrying capital assets, then disposing of capital gains."

Hassana strutted over in his direction, with each step she took, she couldn't stop her voluptuous breasts from jiggling. He couldn't help but occasionally glance. Before reaching him, she closed her blazer and reached over him. She clicked a button and Lady Plus popped on the screen ass naked in the shower.

"Oh, excuse me," Hassana smirked and continued to stroke a few keys on the keyboard.

Antwan sunk into his seat embarrassed.

"You really need to get with today's technology. Everything is accessible on the new software, I had installed for you last month."

"I'm old school. Don't have time to learn all this new gadget stuff."

"I see. Next time turn off your webcam." She motioned toward the webcam off switch. "Then backtrack your log out and erase files. Hit this button, then hold those two down. You don't want to trash them because somebody could go inside your trash and see *everything* you're doing. This way, *nobody* can see what you don't want them to see.

"Thanks…don't ju…"

11

"Mr. Mitchell, your business, in your business, is your business. I work for you. Be back in thirty minutes with lunch. I'll lock the door behind me."

"Here please throw this rabbit food away. My client will be here within an hour. I have to get those numbers together and I don't want to be disturbed.

"No problem, I'll just give you a beep when I return with our lunch." Hassana exited his office, locked the door and double checked to make sure it was locked.

Antwan fumbled around with his assignment for a few minutes but couldn't get the sight of Lady Plus in the shower out his head. He clicked on her site and turned on his webcam. To his surprise but not his dismay he found her oiling up in a wall-sized mirror. Her skin glowed as each speck of oil cascaded across her fudge brown complexion.

Soft sexual moans spilled from her full lips, each time she massaged the strawberry and cream scented oil, into her humungous breasts. Her milk dud like nipples deliciously sat hard, and erect, sending warm, tingling, sensations from the tip of her nipples, through her gut, down to her love box, with each touch.

Antwan continued to stroke the length of his long, thick, dick imagining her tasty nipples between his lips.

Lady Plus retrieved her trustee bullet from its velvet knapsack. She lubricated her bestie with her own spit. She licked the sides, staring into the camera. Her almond shaped dark brown eyes became fixated on the size of Antwan's dick. Her neatly shaped eyebrows and long dazzling eyelashes showed the time and effort of enhancing one's beauty.

"You ready to make this pussy come?"

"Let me see her."

Lady plus adjusted the camera and sat on the floor. His screen showed her freshly shaved, phat, but small size pussy up close and personal. Juices dripped from her overlapping lips, inviting her bestie.

"Umm…" She slid the tip of her bullet inside her Love Box. "Talk dirty to me, Daddy Long Stroke. You know how I like it."

"Give me that pussy. You think you can handle all this dick? Huh, come on go faster."

She followed his orders, stroking her love box fast and hard. She rotated her hips, winding her waist fast and hard, meeting her fast stroke. She used her other hand to open her swollen lips with her index and ring fingers, while her middle finger rapidly stroked her flaming clit as her bestie danced inside her womb.

"Yes, Daddy Long Stroke! Give me all that dick! Right there, make this pussy cum. You…you gone cum on my face?"

"Nah, big mama, I'm going to spray this round all over those mountain size breasts of yours."

"Umm…you nasty, Daddy Long Stroke. I'm going to lick my girls clean from that sweet cum of yours. Ah… Ah… yeah…yeah. You ready, Daddy Long Stroke?"

"Yeah…um huh, come on.

Lady Plus squirted all over the camera lens, causing Antwan to grab a baby wipe to catch his load. He stood up and stroked his hard dick to the sight of Lady Plus's thick, wet tongue licking her own cum from the screen. She adjusted the camera one more time, as she licked her bullet clean as well.

"You want some more, Daddy Long Stroke? My ass hole feels neglected."

"Nah, love, I have work to do."

"Well, go get that money. You know how to find me. I'm only one click away.

Antwan turned off the webcam and followed the instructions he'd gotten from Hassana before he turned off the computer and went to the bathroom to clean up.

CHAPTER TWO

The thirty-minute drive from his office on Market Street, to their home in Carolina Beach, was a much-needed commute. Antwan navigated his Audi A8 through traffic, drumming his finger against the steering wheel to the sound of *'Avant's* 4 *Minutes'*. At barely thirty years old, Antwan had a profound interest in R&B. Something he'd gained a passion for in High School. Right after graduation he submitted to Kim's plead for marriage. She was afraid that if they didn't make that commitment in front of the Lord before they went their separate ways for college, their relationship might not withstand the distance.

As always Kim got her way. They had a small wedding and went off to school. Kim enrolled in UCLA with a full academic scholarship, majoring in Political Science. Antwan stayed close to home and committed to Duke, where he majored in Accounting and Business, giving him room to still be hands-on with the family's business in his free time.

Antwan pulled into his driveway. Freshly manicured lawns decorated the neighborhood. His custom-built home was the biggest and most modern house on the block. The see-through home revealed the sun sitting behind the oceans view just a few yards away from their back patio, and his custom designed speedboat. You would think a man with a master's in business, his own Accountant Firm, a beautiful wife, a lovely home and a dream boat would be happier.

Yet, his sexual frustration wouldn't allow happiness to rest in his heart and mind. He hadn't cheated on his wife physically since college.

Supporting her decision to get gastric bypass surgery, breasts, hip, and ass reductions was the hardest part of their marriage thus far. His undying love for Kim was destroying him internally. Lately, he'd not only had been yearning for his full-figured plus size beautiful wife back, but he also needed more. The fire of his sexual desire burned rapidly. He needed *more action…more sex…more oral…more woman*! One who was willing to explore both of their sexual imaginations and fill up both of their appetites.

Antwan took a deep breath before he exited his car. Kim's Land Rover indicated she was home. He struggled with the sight of Lady Plus's endless curves bent over, throwing her juicy pussy back at the 12-inch dildo she stuck on the wall, with its sticky suction base bottom. His dick got hard at the thought of her thick bottom lip shivering from pleasure.

He entered his lovely home and was engulfed with the familiar fragrance of passion fruit scented candles. To his surprise he found Kim elegantly positioned on a bar stool, with her legs crossed discreetly flashing a sizeable amount of her bare, bright-yellow thigh, peeking from underneath the flare of her silk designer robe. A bottle of wine sat ajar accompanied with two glasses. Her small manicured hands twisted and popped the cork, then began to fill the glasses resting on the L-shape marble counter. Using no words, she ordered him to have a seat by pushing his filled glass towards the open stool next to her.

Antwan placed his leather stylish briefcase on top of the counter and began peeling off his tailor-made suit jacket. Kim couldn't help but admire his broad shoulders, and lean muscular arms bulging out of his dress shirt as he loosened his tie.

He stood 6'1, had caramel-brown skin, dark-brown eyes, a perfect posture and a great texture of hair, that women look for when scouting a baby daddy. He bent over and placed a greeting kiss on her soft heart shaped lips. She met his gesture with a surprisingly passionate embrace, as she slid her tongue into his partly opened mouth! Her warm, wet tongue tasted like chocolate and Moscato. Her sexual desire was told by her eyes and soft moans that escaped her tasty lips.

Kim couldn't help but notice the instant bulge in his pants. Just knowing she was still wanted by the man of her dreams set her flaming pussy on fire. She stalked the way he sipped from the glass. The tip of his thick, strong, tongue poked from his lips, like the head of a spear, greeting the rim of the glass. Envy invaded her mind, wishing her pussy was that glass. It had been months since his tornado tongue demolished her neatly groomed pussy. He used to feast on her goodies for breakfast, lunch, and dinner. Now he barely devoured her perky breasts when they had sex.

"So, what did I do to earn so much attention, by such a beautiful woman?"

"I just felt the need to show my loving husband, he's appreciated and adored."

"Well, thank you, Darling! Give me some sugar." Antwan leaned over and engaged in another passionate kiss.

Afterward, Kim stood up and began massaging his massive shoulders. Antwan closed his eyes and started doing his breathing exercises.

"You know those magical, soft hands will feel a whole lot better without this shirt."

"Your wish is my command." Kim unbuttoned his shirt and peeled him out of it. He had no idea that massaging his bare brown skin, and hard muscles felt better to her as well.

She slid her tiny soft hands up the coast of his arms, as he rested his head on her soft, perfectly round breasts. She ran her freshly manicured fingernails across the fraternity symbol branded in his arm. Her fingers pressed tightly against both of his back arms, making small circles around the huge horseshoe poking out of his arm. By the time she made it to his neck, drool nearly escaped his lips. Her hands always managed to produce a peaceful feeling that sleep followed.

"You can't go to sleep on me tonight." Kim began massaging his scalp, while lightly gliding her fingernails from his always clean shape up, to the back of his neck. His body jerked from the sensation. The hairs on the back of his neck began to rise, along with his dick that pressed against his pants.

Antwan stood, towering over his wife. The look in her pretty hazel-brown eyes was all the ambition he needed. In one swift move, he scooped her small frame in the air, placing her on top of the L-shape counter. He snatched the belt off her silk robe, which instantly untied, exposing her newly sculpted breasts. Not as big as he desired, but soft enough to feed his appetite. Antwan cuffed one of her breasts in his big strong hands and placed her swollen erect nipple into his mouth.

"Umm…wait, not right here." Kim moaned while Antwan attempted to ignore her request.

He twirled his tongue around her nipple and sucked harder just the way she liked. Kim's head dropped back, as she arched her back. It had been so long since she felt his lips on her breasts.

"Ummm… hubby, take me to the bedroom. Not right here the neighbors can see us."

"That's my point," Mumbled Antwan, as he unbuckled his belt.

"I don't want…ohhh…yesss!" Before she could protest Antwan had slipped off her panties and inserted the tip of his hard dick inside of her juicy, phat pussy.

Kim reached up, wrapped her arms around him and squeezed him tight. Her strong embrace matched the grip she placed around his dick. Regardless of her size, Kim's pussy always snapped back to a tight, wet box, that erupted with warm fluids each time they had sex. Antwan braced himself. The length of his long, fat, dick stretched her small, tight pussy as she buried her face in the nape of his neck.

Slowly but forcefully, he stroked her box with passionate magical strokes. Kim wrapped her legs around him when he began to change the direction of his stroke. He dipped low, digging deep into the bottom of her treasure before coming up strong, and repeating the same action.

"Ohhh…yesss, hubby. Ummm, yes, right…right…right there!" Out of breath Kim held on for dear life. As usual, Antwan did all the work.

Well aware of her spot he felt the warm, sticky cum exit her love box as always when he went digging for gold. Her cum soaked his nut sack, as he banged against her tunnel. Long, deep, strong strokes seemed to never end. By the reaction of her body language. Kim was no longer fully interested. She'd come twice, now all she wanted was for Antwan to cum. Being that it had been some time since they had sex, she wondered why he hadn't come yet.

Antwan felt the disconnection. He began to speed up his stroke. Her lack of passion was bothering him considerably. He unlocked her arms from his neck and legs from his waist. He pulled out quickly, leaving her pussy leaking with her wetness. He turned her around and flipped her robe up. Her perfectly round ass spread across the table. In one quick motion, Antwan rubbed the head of his dick up and down the slit of her pussy. Purposely brushing against her swollen clit. The fire in her box began to flame. Kim twirled her ass around, pumping the air. He slammed his big, long dick inside her.

"Ooh, why you…"

Antwan grabbed a hand full of her long hair.

"Stop…stop…get off my hair!"

Antwan shook his head. He wrapped his strong hands around her waist, pinning her down on the table and stroked her pussy hard and fast. No love Strokes, she wanted him to finish and he just wanted to cum.

"You…you hurting meee!"

Frustration overtook his mind. All he could think of was Hassana. How if it was her bent over the table, and how he would be able to do whatever he wanted. He closed his eyes, stroking harder.

"Stop…stop…it, it hurts!" cried Kim.

Antwan sped up, to his surprise he envisioned Hassana. His dick got harder. The strokes were no longer rushed and painful. He slid his hand underneath her and stroked her clit and pussy to the same sync.

Kim stopped crying, her pussy devoured the attention. The sound of his stomach smacking against her ass cheeks turned her on. Antwan felt the tingle in his sack. Not wanting to pull out, he stroked her faster, deeper and stronger. He buried his dick inside her wet pussy.

Kim understood exactly what was going on. "Don't…don't cum."

"Aghhh…" Antwan released his load inside of her then collapsed on her back as he pumped the last bit of semen inside her.

"Why did you do that?"

Antwan began to grind on her some more. His dick was still semi-hard. He was ready for round two.

"No, get off me!" Kim pushed back. She turned around and mugged him as if he did something wrong.

"What?" Antwan asked, standing there stroking his huge cock.

"I thought we decided not to have kids yet? I told you I'm not ready."

"We didn't decide nothing. *We* never do! You decided since you just got this new body, our dreams of having a family had to be put on hold."

"I can't believe you came inside me. What am I supposed to do now?" Kim stormed off to the bathroom.

Antwan fixed his clothes and headed to the shower downstairs. He was confused about everything that had just happened.

CHAPTER THREE

The afternoon sunshine beamed endlessly across the sky, as the ocean view scenery was meant to relieve all stress. Three beautiful women sat alongside the balcony of Fort Fisher's restaurant sipping Martini's. Their morning was spent swiping credit cards shopping at Mayfair.

Kim found herself being nudged by Crystal. "Girl, what's been up with you? You been so distant all day."

"Crystal, you have no idea," Kim replied.

"Then you need to inform us, maybe we do have an idea, if you tell us," informed Lakeisha.

Kim took a deep breath. "I think my marriage is falling apart."

"Why, Antwan cheating?" Lakeisha asked.

"Hush, Lakeisha, let her talk."

"Thanks, Crystal, no, he's not cheating. Well, I don't think he's cheating. It's me, last night we had sex. After he came inside me, I chastised him about it. I said I didn't want to have a baby, right now.

"Why would you? You just got the body of your dreams," interrupted Lakiesha selfishly.

"We did agree that once both of our careers were up and running we would make a family. More importantly, I took a Plan B pill. I've been taking them for the last couple of months even when he does pull out. I'm just not ready to lose my shape. I was miserable when I was heavy. You two remember?" cried Kim.

"Aww don't worry, Antwan will understand. If it's one thing we all know, is how much that man loves you," assured Crystal.

"Don't take that man's love for granted. I'm telling you now. If he wants kids, give him all the kids he wishes. You don't want him stepping out on you, then you're playing step mommy. Gurl, I love Dawan, and those kids, but every time I look at them, I can't help but think of him stepping out on me. I'm not stupid, he's rich, so I'm not leaving, but it does hurt."

Tears rolled down Kim's face. The thought of Antwan cheating and having a family with somebody else hurt her heart.

"Look, Lakiesha, you had to make her cry with all your mess! Kim, just go see my doctor. He'll give you an I.U.D., that will give you time to make up your mind. In the meantime, don't argue or say anything if it happens again. I've had the ring for two years, Marcus has no idea."

"Yeah, but, you guys already have kids, both of y'all. Isn't it my duty as his wife to bear his children?"

"Yes, darling, it is, but when you're good and ready." Answered Crystal as she raised her glass and cheered. "To secrets!"

Thirty Minutes Away, Downtown…

The lights were dim, music smoothly snuck through the nearly empty strip club. The smell of a freshly cleaned area gave off the impression like *'Crazy Horse'* was about to close. This was the furthest from the truth. Antwan made his way to his favorite seat as inconspicuous as possible, tucked away in a little corner, where he could observe incoming traffic and had a front row seat of the stage. He checked his watch for the time. In about seven minutes his secret crush was about to enter the stage.

He noticed at least a dozen men and one woman spread out around the club. Some attended to their conversations as if this lunch hour special was just a business meeting. From the looks of the crowd's attire, they all worked in the corporate world, besides the two young thugs dressed in skinny jeans and tight t-shirts. Antwan locked eyes with a familiar face. A man who always seemed to be here at this time.

Antwan gave him a slight nod of acknowledgment which led to the man returning the gesture. Suddenly, Antwan started to wonder if the man had some type of connection with his secret crush. Was he her lover? Was he a friend of hers? Or better yet did he share the same admiration for this woman as he did?

The door continued to constantly open and close. The crowd doubled in size. More working-class men rushed to their seats with drinks in their hand. Antwan impatiently tapped his foot on the floor. He peeked at his watch again. Not only did he need to get back to his office, before his client arrived, more importantly, he also needed his fix. His thoughts were interrupted.

"What up, Ant?"

"James, what you doing here?"

"Just came from the office. Hassana said you stepped out for a minute. Realized it was Thursday and there was only one place you could be."

A familiar tune burst through the speakers. The crowd erupted in cheers, whistles, and claps, as the hypnotizing melody of the track to Sza's *'Weekend'* had them all on edge.

"Now coming to the stage. Our very own, The Big…The Beautiful…The confident…Tropical Storm!

Three Hundred plus, packed in all thighs, hips, ass, breasts and more ass, glided across the stage demanding everyone's attention. With each strut her confidence shined, mesmerizing the crowd. Her waist almost looked invisible because of her huge breasts, ass, and thighs. No giggle, No sag, No Fupa! Her body seemed flawless. The lights beamed down on her soft French vanilla skin. She batted her kinky slanted eyes at the crowd.

With a slight sway of her hips, she mimicked the popular hoopla dance of her culture. Her Hawaiian descendant portrayed an erotic appearance. Tropical Storm began to rotate her huge ass to the sound of the beat. The music came to a halt, but the beat kept playing. Her ass cheeks bounced loud and clear as she popped up and down on her toes, showing her god given talent. Soon as the beat dropped she bounced to the floor in a full split. The crowd went crazy as she continued her dance routine.

"So, you just can't get enough of her, huh?"

"Sssh… James, cool out. The best part is coming up."

"Ant, I just don't get it. You have a beautiful wife at home." James shook his head, after realizing Antwan wasn't paying him any attention.

Tropical Storm had slipped off her panties. Her juicy pink pussy stared at the crowd. With two strokes from her soft hands, her clit stuck out. Antwan wished James wasn't sitting next to him. He ran his hand back and forth on the length of his dick, through his pants. Tropical Storm spun around on all fours. She cat-crawled across the stage while whipping her long blonde wig, like a crazed white girl. Without warning, she flipped over into a headstand. Once she was fully balanced, she began to move her thighs and ass.

"So, are you going to tell me how you can be so invested in big gurls, with a beautiful wife at home?"

"How many times are you going to refer to my wife as beautiful?"

"You know what I mean. She's just perfect…smart, beautiful, good job. It's hard for a brother to find a good woman nowadays."

"Perfect to who?" Antwan pulled out his wallet and retrieved a picture. He glanced down to make sure it was the right one, then passed it to James. "That's why?"

"Who this big gurl in the picture with you? Oh shit! Hold on is that Kim?"

Antwan snatched the picture and placed it back inside his wallet. Tropical Storm began to play with her pussy.

"Damn, Ant! So, this thing for big women is not just a phase then huh?"

"I love big, beautiful women. See dudes like you think them skinny narrow body woman whose ass bones crush your pelvis when you hit it from the back is sexy. You see all that, right there. I could pound away and watch nothing, but tilde waves form in her ass when I hit that from the back."

"Ha, Ha, Ha! So, if you got it all figured out, why did Kim lose all that weight. She knows you love big women?"

"Because she's selfish. Enough of that, watch the show." Kim's attitude along with his sexual thoughts of Hassana called for a cold shower.

CHAPTER FOUR

Tamia's soft voice secretly expressed how Kim really felt inside *'Stranger in My House'* was a true statement. Antwan hadn't been coming home at his regular time, nor had they had sex since that incident three weeks ago. Kim stood at the mirror fixing her make-up, as the front door opened and closed.

Antwan rushed in. "Good to see you're getting ready. We have to be at the event in thirty minutes," He explained while stripping out of his clothes and turning on the shower.

"What event are you talking about? I'm going to Crystal's sister's engagement party." Kim couldn't help but gush her panties at the sight of Antwan's naked body through the mirror. His long, thick dick just swung back and forth with each movement.

"Kim, I told you months ago we had the Black Lives Matter Event this weekend. It's on the calendar!"

"You haven't said, but maybe three words to me in weeks. How was I supposed to remember? I don't even have anything to wear. Plus, I can't disappoint Crystal she's my friend."

Antwan shook his head as the warm water cascaded down his back, and he took a deep breath. He wanted to say, *'I thought, I was your husband and your best friend?'* Instead, he lathered his rag and washed up.

"Hubby…what are you going to do? I can't just go to something like that without having my stylist hook me up."

"Don't worry about it, Sweetheart. I'll figure this out, go on to the party. Tell the young lady I said congratulations."

Kim slid the shower door open. Her low glossy eyes told Antwan what she was thinking. He quickly rinsed off and reached for his towel.

"Hold up. You got time for a quickie, right now? I'll let you bend me over the sink real fast. Just don't mess up…"

"Your hair…I know you, never want me to pull or touch your hair. Thanks, but I don't really have the time." Antwan pushed pass her standing beside the shower.

Kim followed him, with her hands on her hip. She couldn't believe he'd turned her down. "You know, you shouldn't still be upset about what happened. We're married, and both have to compromise with each other."

"I'm not thinking about what happened. You don't want to have my kids. Well at least not, right now. Your body is more important than my happiness and dreams. Cool, have it your way… like always."

"You're a jerk. You don't have to say it like that. You know that's not what I meant."

Antwan stood there, ass naked and lotioning up. He purposely stroked his penis with both hands and moisturized his nut sack. He caught Kim just starring. Witnessing the look on her face, only made him smile on the inside. All the times he wanted her, and she didn't comply. He teased her for a few more minutes then got dressed.

Hustamore Housing Projects

Hassana exited her red brick home looking like a runway model. She had on a gray silky gown, that was see-through in the cleavage area, it matched the white and gray streaks in her jet-black hair. Her designer shoes added spunk to match her hair. Spikes, straps, and buckles accommodated her 6-inch Red Bottoms. The crowd of young hustlers stopped what they were doing and caught a glimpse of the woman, that all of them had been crushing for. Nobody from the projects had managed to get in those panties. That was partly why they mean mugged Antwan while he starred at Hassana with his mouth wide open.

"You look beautiful."

"Thanks, glad you called. I always wanted to go to this event."

Antwan opened the car door for her. "You smell wonderful as well."

"Thanks, it's my own special mixture. I don't want other women smelling or looking like me."

"I'm sure you'll be the apple of every man's eye tonight."

"Are you flirting with me, Mr. Mitchell?"

"My name is Antwan tonight, and you're my date for the evening. Aren't I supposed to compliment and flirt with you? Unless you don't feel comfortable."

"No, no, I feel comfortable—real comfortable," Hassana stated and couldn't help but blush.

City Hall Castle Street

"Black Lives Matter!"

"Black Lives Matter!"

Outside the event was filled with protestors. A swarm of people stood outside with bullhorns, banners, and t-shirts, bearing the faces of numerous young black men who were *unjustifiably* killed by law enforcement. Being a pillar of his community, Antwan was a guest speaker. He voiced his opinion on how the youth should be heard and understood, so the community would know how to help them. Stating education and unconditional love should be the first steps to change.

Before he was done, the crowd was misty-eyed and shaking their heads in agreement. Afterward, an elite group including his date Hassana went out for drinks and dancing. The way they finished each other's sentences, laughed at each other's jokes and tore up the dance floor, many questioned their employee...employer relationship. There was a twinkle in their eyes when they looked at one another. Not wanting the night to end they found themselves at a hotel enjoying more of each other's company.

"Oh, yes...yes! Pull my hair, I love it like that!" Hassana spread her wide, soft, bubble ass cheeks for Antwan to dig as deep as possible.

The Cognac had his dick so hard, it hurt. The sound of her juices splashing against his stomach only made them more excited. Beads of sweat cascaded down her milk chocolate skin. He sunk his huge hands into her soft humongous ass cheeks. He was amazed at how well proportionate her figure was. At five-eight, she packed her two-hundred and twenty-five pounds into her tight frame.

"Take this dick! You like long strokes?" He asked while he clutched a fist full of her hair, pulling his eleven-inch dick out of her until just the tip was in, then he forcefully rammed each inch inside her flaming wet pussy.

"Umph…damn! Yes, fuck this pussy…spank me! Come on, babe, spank this coochie!" Hassana took every stroke like a pro. She reached under them and massaged his huge balls with her soft hands.

"Or you like short, fast deep strokes?" Antwan bounced in and out of her, which caused her mouth to get stuck open as words tried to escape.

She answered by grinding back on him whenever he deep stroked her hot box. To his surprise, Hassana started making her ass clap on his dick. He remembered Lady Plus had made her ass do that same trick and wondered how it would feel. And like he thought, it felt great. Not only did Hassana make her ass cheeks swell and shrink, becoming bigger and smaller with each motion. Her pussy muscles tightened and loosened to the same rhythm. She looked back at him. Now his mouth was the one that was wide open.

She purposely slammed back into him. Antwan nearly fell off the bed. His dick came out, and before he could return Hassana turned around. She pushed him to the side making him lie on his back. Her small hands gripped his hard dick. She worked him with both hands, squeezing and jerking in different directions. Her wet mouth slurped on the head of his swollen cock.

Her head bobbed up and down, all side jaw. She looked him in his eyes, spit on his dick, and licked around his head. Her tongue felt like wet silk. She removed her hands and licked the vein of his dick, then took him into her mouth. Drool spilled from the side of her mouth.

"Damn, this dick taste good. I've wanted to suck your dick ever since my first day at work."

"Yeah, what took you so long?"

"Good things happen to those who wait." Hassana started going crazy on his dick.

Foam packed the side of her mouth, as snot dripped from her nose. She started growling and grunting and sucking his dick like a mad woman. Before Antwan could resist he came in her mouth, but she didn't stop. She swallowed all his cum and sucked him until he was hard again.

"Come on…ride this dick."

"Thought you'd never ask." She crawled on top of him and guided his long thick dick, into her dripping pussy.

"You feel tight like I never been inside you before."

"You like the way I feel?"

"Yeah!" Antwan leaned upward, took her large breasts into his mouth-watering lips.

Her breasts tasted sweet. She must have bathed in that special scent she wore. Every part of her body tasted and smelled sweet…even her sweat. Hassana wrapped her arms around his muscular back. She worked him up and down, slow and steady. She wanted to make love to his dick. The way he stroked her back, gripping her ass, and forced her down on each inch, told her he wanted the same. It wasn't rough, or soft, instead, it was passionate, sexy, and fulfilling. He licked her breast with caution, sucking her nipples soft. His wet, warm, thick tongue lapped her other breast hungrily.

"Umm…that one…that's the one!" Hassana moaned.

She held her head back, rotating her hips in small circles every time her love box came down on his length. Her grinds were met by his hook, stroking the side of her walls endlessly. He pulled her hair back, making her look to the ceiling. He kissed on her and bit her on the chin. She squeezed him tighter, grinding harder. Her swollen clit rubbed against the friction of his pelvic area. He pushed back balls deep.

"I'm…I'm wooo…yes, I'm cum…woo…yes! I'm cumminn…"

Antwan's toes curled, he gripped her ass cheeks harder as she bounced up and down, grinding into his nuts. Her pussy soaked the bed sheets. He could hardly breathe, as she held him tight. She squeezed the muscles of her pussy making sure she drained him of every drop of cum. Antwan clasped backward, with her in his arms. He was sweating and breathing hard with his chest heaving up and down as they both tried to catch their breath.

"You ready for some more," he asked.

"Yeah, but I want to suck that sweet dick of yours first."

Antwan closed his eyes thinking there must be a sex God because Hassana was everything he'd ever dreamed of.

CHAPTER FIVE

The doctor's office was elegantly designed from its brass chairs, marble desk, to its variety of crystal vases, seemingly decoder with beautiful fresh arrangements. An antique grandfather clock sat counter cornered in the waiting room. Kim couldn't help but watch time tick away. It was all happening to slow for her. Crystal gossiped about something, yet, Kim didn't hear a word she said. All she hoped was that the doctors would call her name before she changed her mind. Her heart ached at the thought of how hurt Antwan would be if he knew what she was doing. Her undying love for him was not the issue. She just couldn't bear the chance of losing her newly sculptured body.

All her life, she was told how beautiful she was for a big girl. Kids use to tease her in middle school because of how thick she was. They called her names like big draws and thunder thighs. She started getting a lot of the wrong attention from the older young men in her neighborhood. This only made the girls her age even more jealous. Kim tried her best to ignore the haters, by burying her head in her studies, yet, Ant wouldn't allow that. He'd always told her how pretty she was. He defended her from the bullies and walked her to and from school regularly until they became an official couple.

"Mrs. Mitchell, the Doctor is ready to see you now."

Kim snapped out of her trip down memory lane. Her feet felt like they were cinder blocks. She was having second thoughts.

"Gurl, it's going to be alright. You can always come back and have them take the I.D.U. out. Shit, my husband's dick so damn big he be banging this shit further up me. I had to come see the doctor because it was damn near in my tubes."

"Crystal that's not making things any better. You know Antwan's hung."

"Well, this is your body and you're trying to enjoy it. You can tell him or wait for his dick to find it on its own."

"I know your right. Plus, I can't keep hiding those Plan B pills. I almost ran out the other day. That's why we had that big ol' fight."

"After this, you can let him cum inside you, and not say a word. Shoot you can even tell him to during sex just to turn him on."

Kim shook her head and entered the doctor's office. She instructed her and Crystal to take a seat, then began explaining how the I.D.U. worked. That it didn't protect them from sexually transmitted diseases, and it wasn't even a guaranteed that she couldn't get pregnant. Still, in all, Kim held hands with Crystal until it was time for her to get the procedure done.

Later On That Evening

Antwan found himself engulfed trying to be prepared for his meeting with this new client. It was imperative that he crossed all T's and dot all I's. The last meeting with Tru Colors Brewing Company went spectacularly. He was amazed at how ninety-eight percent of the employees were gang members of rival gangs. They put their differences aside, to bring in a decent amount of revenue, and helped stop the violence in their community.

Kim peeked in his home office. "Hubby are you busy?"

Antwan ignored her question, thinking it was obvious. Kim crept in, not caring if she interrupted him. Come on Hubby, it's been over a month and you not only haven't touched me, but you barely speak sentences over four words."

"Kim, I'm busy."

"Even things like that. You been calling me, Kim. What happened to darling, baby or beautiful?"

"Not right now, Darling." Antwan didn't even look up at her.

He kept his head down, purposely avoiding her. It was not so much of him being upset with her for not wanting to have his baby. It was more so the guilt of him cheating on his wife. Eleven years of marriage, and besides that one time in college, this was really his first time physically cheating on her. The sad part was he loved every minute of it.

"Can you look at me…please? We need to talk," Kim demanded.

"What…what do you want?" He slammed down his pen, and for the first time looked up at Kim.

She stood there pouting, which only turned him on. Her pretty little-freckled nose flared. Those sexy brown eyes gawked down at him.

"I want you to forgive me. I want us to work this out. I want peace in my home!"

"And I want a baby. I want to start a family with my wife. I want for once in this relationship for it not to always be about what you want."

Kim's mouth couldn't close if she placed it inside a vice grip. "What do you mean?" She crossed her arms under her breasts unintentionally pushing them up.

As much as Antwan wanted to be upset with her, he desired the need to penetrate her water wall. Just to shake the addiction he felt coming on for Hassana's freaky self.

"What do I mean?" He pushed his chair back.

"This is what I mean. Take those leggings off and sit down on my desk, so I can eat your pussy."

"Huh?" Kim was completely caught off guard.

The heat and steam that was once coming from her head was now down to her box! A warm wet gape of moisture seeped through her leggings. Antwan noticed her nipples getting erect. She stood there in shock.

"Come here! You heard what I said." He tugged at her arm. She didn't resist, instead, she listened.

"I can't believe you're talking to me like that." Pulling off the other leg of her leggings.

She walked over to his desk, timid and nervous, yet aroused. She could count on one hand how many times he took the dominant role.

Kim set on his desk uneasy. Antwan placed her feet on his thighs. He spread her legs at the kneecap. A light runway patch of her dirty red pubic hair displayed her fresh trim. He couldn't help it. He shook his head knowing he told her over and over, he likes it bald. Part of him just wanted to stop, but her juicy, fat, pretty, pussy called him.

He placed soft kisses from her left kneecap, up her inner thigh. The closer he got the kisses turned to licks. He ran his tongue up the slit of her box, tasting her sweet juices.

"Umm!" Kim moaned, enjoying his touch. It had been so long.

Antwan licked on her clit, before he took it in his mouth, sucking slow, kissing, then licking it again just the way she loved. He used both hands to spread her pussy open. Her pussy lips were so fat, he decided on a French kiss. Kissing and sucking both sides, then slipping his tongue as deep inside as possible. He twirled his tongue around the inside of her pussy, enjoying the taste of her nectar.

"Oh, yes…yes! I miss you…I miss this!"

Antwan began to breath harder. Her moans only ignited the beast in his pants. The louder she moaned the wetter her pussy poured. Antwan blew into her box, then on her clit. Kim's body shivered as he sucked her clit with intense passion.

"Hubby!" Nearly out of breath, she rubbed his waves, pushing her pussy into his mouth.

She raised her hips off the desk, grinding her pussy on his face. Antwan couldn't help but smirk. She had no problem throwing it back when he gave her oral, yet while having intercourse she'd usually just lie there. He unfastened his belt to release the beast. He attempted to remove his face from her box. Kim squeezed her thighs together, and pushed the back of his head, still grinding on his face.

Antwan stroked his rock, hard thick, long, dick, as he slurped her soaked sweet pussy, with his skillful tongue. He unlocked her hands, with his free hand, muscled his way out of her strong thigh grip. As he stood, Kim let out a frustrated moan. She would prefer he just ate her pussy until she came. That was what he'd asked.

Antwan lubricated the tip of his dick with her juices. The tightness of her tunnel had always felt homely. Now he found himself out of place. He placed one of her legs on his shoulder and eased his dick inside her flowing tunnel.

"Owww…ssst, wait…go slow." Kim wined.

Realizing it had been months since they'd had sex, and Kim always had that snap back, Antwan pumped in and out of her real slow. With each stroke, he forced his way deeper inside her pussy. Like magic, her tunnel opened for his entrance. He began to speed up his strokes.

"You missed this dick?"

"Yes…ohh, yes!"

"Yeah, tell me how much you missed it." He began to make wide circles inside her pussy.

She removed her leg from his shoulder and wrapped both legs around him. She pushed the heels of her feet into his ass cheeks, forcing him to go deeper.

"Oh yes…I miss it. I miss it sooo…much please give me all of it. I love…I love you, Hubby!" Kim wept.

Antwan had found her spot. He banged against her insides using his half-circle stroke. Her bottom lip shivered as he wrapped his huge hands around her waist, forcing her to throw it back. He controlled her movement long enough for her to understand what he wanted. She began to rotate her hips, throwing it back on her own. Antwan couldn't help but become more excited.

He sucked on her shivering bottom lip, then stuck his tongue down her throat. Kim tried to turn away as if she didn't want to taste herself on his tongue, Antwan wouldn't allow that. In his mind, he realized she'd never satisfy him completely.

He removed himself from her grip. Turned her around and bent her over his desk. He placed his forearm on her lower back and gripped one of her ass cheeks.

"Smack!"

"Ouch, what are you doing?"

"Trying to make that ass jiggle."

"Let me make it feel better." He massaged her soft ass cheek as a devilish grin spread across his face.

If only she could see him. He entered her from behind, ramming his length inside.

"Ooowwww…why?"

Antwan rammed himself in and out of her fast and hard. She reached behind and tried to place her hand on his chest to stop him from hurting her.

"Why…ooowww…ouchh! Hubby…Hubby why."

Antwan removed her hand. He reached for her hair but hesitated, knowing she'd bitch and complain. Instead, he decided to stick his thick index finger in her anal.

"Hol…hold up, Hubby. No…unh…unh!"

"Sssh…I got you, relax. Remember no more traditional."

"Oh…oh…okay, just go slow."

He smiled inside and out and slowed up his strokes. Using the rhythm of his finger in her ass as a guide to swing his wand. He peeked over Kim's shoulder. Her eyes were closed, and drool leaked from the side of her mouth. Instantly her legs began to shake uncontrollably. Her pussy was so wet, it began to fart.

"Oh, shit…oh shit! Hubby…Hubby, oh Hubby…I'm cumming Hubby. I'm cumming hard…what you. What you doing to meee…"

A river of fluids poured from both her anal and pussy at the same time. The sign of her climax only made him release his load at the same time. He dug inside her balls deep and exploded. He held it there, squirting every drop into her. Once they caught their breaths he just knew she was going to fuss over him cumming inside her. To his surprise, she looked back.

"You finish…it's all out?"

"Yeah, I'm good." He pulled out.

"No, wait. Leave it right there. My coochie hurt, but I don't want you out of me yet. That might be the baby, you want right there."

"Huh…so, you're not mad?" Antwan had to pull out and sit in his chair. She'd just threw him a curveball.

"No, you're my husband. The love of my life, and if you're ready for that family, I promise, so am I." she lied.

He turned her around, pulled her onto his lap and kissed her a few times.

"I love you!"

"I love you too, Hubby!"

"So, you ready for another round?"

"Oh no. But, I'll go make you something to eat. By the way, what made you think of putting your finger in there? You been watching nasty movies?"

"Why you didn't like it?"

"Not at first, but it was different. I think I came out of my you know what."

"You did."

Kim strutted away on cloud nine, assured that everything was back to normal with their marriage. So, what she'd lied, he'd never know.

CHAPTER SIX

"Mr. Mitchell, you have a Mr. B-Fresh out here. I believe he's your two-thirty-five appointment."

"Send him in Hassana. Thank you!"

A few seconds later, in walked his client. He was dark skin, standing five-six, with cornrows, tattoos all over his face and a prison diddy-bop that only came from years of walking the big yard.

"Mr. B-Fresh, glad you could make it. Please have a seat."

"The pleasure's all mines. Pardon the delay, it's been kind of hectic lately. I just opened up my second location for, *'Dripping With Ink.'* Plus, the record label, *'Double Money Entertainment'* has been booking a lot of out of town shows."

"Yeah, well congratulations. I've read about your story on how you went from selling drugs, gang banging and being a violent criminal, to running two of the most lucrative businesses in Wilmington."

"Yeah, I love the Port. It's Port Bity over everything. Me and my homies came a long way."

"Speaking of your homies. I was at the *'Black Lives Matter'* event and had the pleasure to meet Mr. Johnson. He was being chaperoned around by the Mayor, who stated that you helped orchestrate the Tru Colors Brewing Company from behind the prison walls. How did you manage that?"

"Well, I didn't really orchestrate anything. The homies found the way. I just kind of influenced others to commit to the movement. More importantly, I'm here to discuss our future business regarding, 'Double Money Entertainment' and 'Dripping With Ink.' My business is very lucrative, and I heard you're very good at what you do.

"Yes, Mr. B-Fresh, I've also heard about your companies and all the contributions you give to the community. So, it would be an honor to assist you in taking both your companies to a whole other level. I took the liberties of checking your books. You're leaving out the opportunity to increase your network by at least two hundred thousand dollars. That's just what I've seen so far. You can see my secretary, she'll inform you of the deposit fee, and we can take it from there. Since I just started being your accountant, I'll have to meet with you every Thursday around four p.m. before closing. Is that a problem?

"Nah, that's cool, but how long do we have to do this? I'm really busy."

"Well, it's important that I go over the books with you. So, I can teach you a few things while I get your approval on certain moves. It should only take four to six weeks. Once a week for maybe an hour, or an hour and a half. When things are up to speed, we'll meet monthly."

"Say no more, I'll leave my deposit out front. I look forward to seeing you next week." B-Fresh rose out of the chair and shook Antwan's hand. He watched Antwan's eyes scan the tats covering his hands and face. His close family and friends were disappointed when he decided to tatt his face with Gang writing. Stating that he would never make it in the Corporate world. Now he was on the verge of becoming one of the most successful young black businessmen in his city.

Later That Evening

The warm night breeze pierced their faces, as mist from the ocean sprinkled micro specks of water on various body parts each time the speedboat splashed against the water's current. Antwan navigated his speedboat through the coast of Carolina. After the successful meeting with B-Fresh, he decided to celebrate. Kim had already committed her time to Lakisha and Crystal like always, while Hassana had been eager for some one on one time.

"It's beautiful out here," Hassana stated as she watched the reflection from the stars dance off the ocean floor.

"I haven't driven my baby in months, been so busy I forget how relaxing this is." Antwan idled the speedboat just far enough off the coast to be out of one's eyesight.

He couldn't help but take in the glimpse of how attractive Hassana looked tonight. Her long curly weave flew effortlessly in the wind. Her canary yellow two-piece and multi-colored see-through wrap around complemented her dark chocolate skin. That ever so hypnotizing fragrance she wore the night of the *'Black Lives Matter'* event had him reminiscing about that wonderful experience.

Hassana decided to break the awkward silent moment. "So…that night…"

"What about it?"

"You never said anything to me about it. We've been back to work as if nothing happened. Let a woman know, was that just a onetime thing? You're back happily married? I know you enjoyed yourself because I'm confident in my work. I just need to know what's next. Tired of sitting at my desk, wondering if you're going to walk up on me and put that tasty big dick in my mouth, or bend me over your desk and spank me."

"Honestly, it's all still a little confusing. I don't want it to be a onetime thing. My marriage is complicated. Of course, I enjoyed myself. Whatever you want to do next is on you. So, if you have a taste for this dick, come get him. If you want to get fucked from behind, bend over, I'll spank you in more ways than one."

"So, what you're about to introduce me to the Tide High Club? I never had sex on a boat in the middle of the ocean."

"Let's scratch that off your bucket list." Antwan took off his captain sailor hat and placed it on Hassana's head.

She wasted no time and immediately dropped to her knees, clawed at his belt buckle, and unleashed his semi-hard dick. She stuck her tongue out and rubbed the head of his dick against the edge of her teeth delicately sending an electric shockwave to his nut sack.

"Hold up."

Hassana ignored his demand and wrapped her long thick, wet tongue around the head of his dick. One hand held the base of his dick, directing his now hard erection to the sky. Her other hand held onto the Captain's hat, so it wouldn't fall. Her tongue jerked off the head of his dick. She peeked up at him and found a satisfying glare, his eyes could barely stay open and his mouth wouldn't close. She took him in her warm, wet, sloppy mouth slurping on his length.

Antwan bent his head back and faced the sky. He opened his eyes, taken by the beautiful purple, blue, and burnt orange sky. The sound of the water splashing against the boat, light whistles of the ocean air, and loud slurping of Hassana spitting and sucking on his dick, created a melody fit for a king. He looked down at the determination in her eyes. He reached down to retrieve his hat, but she smacked his hand away and gave him an evil stare. Antwan couldn't help but be extremely turned on by her aggressiveness.

"Stand up, it's time for that spanking."

Hassana popped his dick out of her mouth. She began to plant soft kisses all over it, as he pulled her to her feet. She displayed enough restraint to let him know she wasn't finished. Once she was on her feet, he planted a wet kiss on her full juicy lips. He wrapped his hands around her sixty-two-inch hips and gripped that huge, soft, wide ass.

"Turn around," he demanded

"Yes, Daddy." She turned around giggling ready for her discipline.

"Take off that wrap."

"You do it."

"Oh, you want to be hard-headed and stubborn?"

"Yup, what you are you going to do about it?"

Antwan understood clearly what she was looking for. It was all a part of her foreplay. He loosened her tie knot. The size of her hips made her thirty-eight waist appear tasteful, for all BBW lovers. The wide gap in her crotch area stopped the top of her thighs from rubbing. Her swollen clit protruded from the thin fabric of her bikini bottom. Antwan couldn't help but run his index finger against her clit.

"Ummm…" Hassana moaned, as his fingers brushed against her lust button.

The heat and moisture between her legs called him. He eased his fingers into the waist of her bikini. He twisted a nice amount around his finger, then balled it into his fist.

"Oucchhh!" Hassana screamed when he ripped her bottom off.

Antwan forced her to bend over. As requested she grabbed both ankles. The sight of her wide, soft, chocolate glistening ass made all the blood rush to the tip of his dick. As he smacked her ass.

"Harder, I've been bad." Hassana begged.

As she requested he smacked her as hard as he could, trying his best not to hurt her too bad.

"Put it in." Hassana wiggled her ass in the air.

Antwan smacked her ass again, even harder this time. "Shut up! You wanted this dick, right?"

"Yes…oh yes! Give me all that long dick daddy!"

Antwan placed his dick in the crack of her ass. She squeezed his cock with the muscles in her ass cheeks. He smacked her on the ass one more time, just to watch the waves.

"Come on put it in...*please*!"

Antwan sunk both hands into the softness of her ass cheeks spread them apart and slid his dick slowly into her tunnel.

"Umm...yes! It feels so good."

"This what you want!"

"No, I want you to fuck me...fuck me hard!"

On-demand he slammed each inch inside her box. The deeper he got the wetter she became. Still holding her ankles Hassana rocked back on her heels, meeting his thrust with her own force. He began to speed up his strokes. He removed his hands from her ass cheeks and wrapped them around her waist. Now he controlled her movement while slamming in and out of her with deep long strokes.

"Yes...yes, ooohhh...yes! Fuck this pussy...give me that dick! Harder...harder!" Hassana no longer gripped her ankles.

She placed her palms down and spread her legs just enough for Antwan to bend a little at the knees, focusing on her g-spot. With each stroke, it felt like a water balloon bussed in her pussy and splashed all over his dick, balls, thighs, and stomach. Never in his life did he think a woman's insides could feel so good.

"I'm cumming...again! Again...oohhhh...yeah! I...I gotta get down. Please...my pussy...it...it hurts!"

"You wanted to get fucked...now take this dick!"

Hassana slowly crawled to the floor. Antwan continued to stroke her pussy, not missing a beat. She was now on all fours. Antwan stood on one knee and punished her with long side strokes.

"Pull my hair…spank me!"

With a fist full of hair and his dick deep inside her pussy, he continuously smacked her ass. Her screams and whimpers were one of lust and satisfaction. Her pussy purred endless love juice, which made his dick even harder. The tip of his dick banged against a spot in her treasure, that caused her to have multiple orgasms for seven minutes straight. Tears rolled down her eyes, low whispers of a language he couldn't understand exited her mouth. Finally, his balls started to boil. She could tell by the hesitation of his stroke, that he was about to cum but didn't want to.

"Fuck this pussy! You hear me…this your pussy! You like this juicy phat pussy"

"Yes…I love it!"

"Fuck her. Don't love her, she been bad…I been bad. Fuck me pleassseee!

Antwan came inside her, as she came again for the fourth time. They collapsed on the deck of the boat out of breath. He rolled over and looked up at the sky. She crawled over and placed her head on his chest.

"Come on, get this thing up. I want to ride the shit out of this big muthafucka."

"Hold up, give me a minute."

"Nah, don't trip…I got this!" Hassana kissed her way down his chest and found her new best friend.

She kissed his dick, then took him into her mouth. She took his hat off and placed it on his head. "My turn." She whispered in his ear after she eased down on all of his dick and went to work.

CHRONICLES OF A BBW

CHAPTER SEVEN

Raindrops danced across the front of Kim's windshield. The late-night patrons scrambled through the downtown streets. Kim drove 10 miles over the speed limit. Her eyes began to tear, as guilt, loneliness, confusion, and defeat filled her heart and mind. She thought the sexual episode her and Antwan shared two weeks ago would've brought them closer. Yet, she hadn't spent any time with him, unless they were sleep, and as far as sex, Antwan hit her with a couple of lazy strokes to crave his early morning hard-on a few days ago. *Keisha Cole's 'I Should of Cheated'*, crept through her speakers.

She pulled over in front of Antwan's firm. After hearing him complain about all the late long hours at work she was suspicious about him spending all those hours with Hassana. She'd heard rumors about them dancing the night away at the *'Black Lives Matter'* event. She'd also called the office on those long late hours to still find Hassana at work as well.

Kim parked her Range and rushed inside the firm. "Where's my husband?" She snapped as she stood over Hassana's desk.

"How you are doing, Mrs. Mitchell?"

"Don't how you doing me. Where's my husband!"

"Excuse me. Hi, what's up, Kim, how you been?"

Kim spun around ready to curse whoever just interrupted her out.

"I've been here for two hours waiting on him."

"Hi, James!" Kim gave him a big hug.

"Like I told, Mr. James. Mr. Mitchell had several meetings at the Mayor's office and should be returning shortly." Hassana grilled Kim. Never wanting to expose her hand, and disrespect her boss's wife, like a jealous side piece. She just wasn't going to let her disrespect her either.

"I'm surprised, you're not with him at City Hall. Heard you two been occupying one another lately." Kim said in an accusatory tone.

James stood there with a perplexed expression on his face. He caught on that Kim was insinuating Antwan had something going on with Hassana. His head swung back and forth as if it was on a swivel.

"Listen, I attended a few work functions with my *Boss*! Honestly, each time I thought you would have been on his arm." Hassana fired back.

"I'll be on his arm the next time you can bet that!" Kim assured.

"Okay, ladies let's all just calm down. Obviously, my main man Ant-Money is not here to defuse or defend the situation. Ms. Hassana stated he's not here and will be here soon. So, come on Kim, we'll just have a seat and catch up on old times." James interrupted, trying to alleviate the tension in the room.

Kim stared a hole in the top of Hassana's head. She was livid at her back talk. She planned to have a long talk with Antwan about her, and the possibility of her being fired. Hassana knew she'd overstepped her boundaries. Everything just came out and she could no longer allow her to talk to her like that. She felt her looking at her but decided to focus on her work and suppress her feelings. She'd already said too much.

"Kim, you're looking beautiful as always." James admired her figure in her skinny jeans, riding boots, and a leather jacket.

"Aggh…I can't believe that lady! Did you see how she poked her chest out at me like I'm in the wrong?" Kim fussed.

"What I saw, was an angry wife basically accusing her husband's secretary of messing around with her boss. I know you don't think Antwan is stupid enough to mess around with that?" He looked in Hassana's direction. "When he has someone as gorgeous as you at home."

Kim finally looked up, she caught the Barry White baritone. "James, are you flirting with me?"

"If I was would you tell Ant?"

The office door swung open. Antwan closed his umbrella and placed it in the can next to the coat rack. He happened to look up while taking off his raincoat. Three sets of eyes peered up at him. Kim's was the first to attack.

"Where you been? Why you never texted me back? Why are you so distant?" Kim rambled off one question after the other.

"Mr. Mitchell, may I please have a few words with you in private?" Hassana stood from the desk, sounding more like she was making a demand instead of a request.

"Ant-Money looks like you got your hands full. Thought I'd remind you about what we discussed. Been here for a minute. Checked all your spots Big and Small, couldn't find you." James stated.

Antwan looked at James. His words didn't do as much damage as seeing him rest his hand on his wife's lower back. When he looked up, Kim's facial expression changed. James nor Kim could see Hassana standing behind them. She cut her eyes at them, then shook her head at Antwan. Then he was the one looking confused. He looked at Kim who stepped away from James and was headed in his direction.

"You really need to have a talk with your secretary. She was just mouthing off at me like I'm not your wife. Is there something going on between you two? Seems like you're spending more time with her than me."

"Kim, I really think you need to go on home. Coming to my place of business, trying to convey indirectly that I'm having an affair is just too much. You have gone too far. I have a few things to handle and I'll be home. We really need to talk!" Antwan stepped toward the door.

"Oh, and James we'll handle that situation tomorrow. You can leave as well."

"No, problem boss man. I didn't mean to intrude. My timing must of been totally off."

"Yeah, must be."

Hassana stood at her desk wondering if Antwan was upset with her. Should she had defended herself? He hadn't look anywhere in her direction yet. She dropped her shoulders in defeat, as nervousness started to set in.

"Damn will he fire me over this? She just asked if we were sleeping together. He didn't answer the question." She watched Kim exit the office door with James a few steps behind her.

"Hassana meet me in my office in five!" Antwan demanded.

He still hadn't looked at her. She plopped down in her seat and tapped her pen against the desk, counting down the minutes.

Meanwhile Outside…

58

"Hey, Kim, hold up. Let me walk you to your car," James offered.

Tears poured down Kim's face, each drop felt like salt water sliding down an open wound. She was upset, embarrassed, confused, and lonely. Antwan had never in all the years they'd been together made her feel so small.

"Kim…Kim, are you alright?" James approached looking concerned.

"Yes, I'm fine." Kim quickly wiped her eyes and tried to fix her face.

"I just wanted to make sure. Is it alright if I walk you to your car?"

"I don't mind."

A few moments of silence passed before James put his plan into action. "That was crazy back there, right?" Kim didn't respond. "I mean do you really think Ant would cheat on you? I mean you're almost perfect."

"I don't know what to think, right now."

"Yeah, well if that's the case he's a damn fool. If by any chance, I had a woman like you, cheating wouldn't even be a thought. No disrespect but your smart, kind and beautiful, with a great career and you're sexy as hell."

"Thanks for the compliment. I work hard to keep my figure!" Kim finally smiled.

"I can see that. What would you say if I asked you out for a drink, just as friends?"

Kim gave him a suspicious look. "You're my husband's friend. Us going out for drinks as just friends or anything else will be totally inappropriate. Yes, I'm an emotional wreck, who may be on the verge of losing my marriage. Yet, I'm still a woman with integrity and morals James."

"Wait, Kim. In no form or fashion do I mean any harm? I just thought you needed a drink or two and someone to listen. It seems like, you're missing someone who enjoys your company."

"I don't know James, it just feels inappropriate." Kim insisted.

"Well, listen, I'm not going to make this situation any more awkward then it is. Here's my card, if you need somebody to talk to or even change your mind about that drink, call me." James helped Kim into her car and watched her pull off. He felt if Antwan didn't want her fine ass, then he would surely take her.

Back Inside The Office...

Hassana's feet felt like they were cinder blocks. Her red bottoms dragged against the carpet, which made the slow walk to Antwan's office seem incapable. She managed to get in front of his door. She took a deep breath and tapped on the door.

"Come in!" Antwan ordered. He sat at his desk calm, fingers interlaced, shoulders straight, his head up and chest out. "Have a seat."

"Mr. Mitchell..." Hassana started to explain but was cut off.

"Ssshhh...just have a seat!" Antwan repeated.

Hassana complied, she felt like she was in middle school and had just got called to the principal's office. "Please don't fire me...I need my job!" she pleaded.

Antwan burst out laughing. "I'm not going to fire you. However, you need to know you can't go toe to toe with my *wife*."

"Honestly, I know better. But, the things she said and how she was acting. Just caused me to lose it. I promise it will not happen again."

"I hope not. In the meantime, I think it will be best for all of us if we took a little break with the personal events."

"I clearly understand. I knew you were married when we started having our *personal events*, as you call them. So, regardless of how I'm starting to feel about you. I have to stay in my lane."

"I would ask you to elaborate on your feelings, but I'm afraid it will not help either of us deal with the much-needed break."

Hassana just shook her head. Antwan was beyond handsome. His dick was huge, and he was so smart it was hard not to wish she was his wife. "So, how long?"

"How long what?" Antwan shrugged.

"How long is the lil' break going to be for? I might want to use some of this vacation time I have left."

"Vacation…how are you going to do that, when we're bringing in more business now than ever?"

She just gave him a blank stare. She wanted to ask him, how could he fuck her so good, lick her ass and pussy last night, and now talk about a break. "I just need to become unattached and ask myself if this is even worth the emotional rollercoaster."

Antwan's tone quickly changed and became more understanding. "I hear you now. Well if that's how you feel. Take all the time off you need, and when you get back tell me if it's worth it."

CHAPTER EIGHT

It had been a little over a month since the whole office debacle. Hassana had just returned to work a week prior. She and Antwan hadn't spoken a word about their affairs. Hassana figured it must have been over. She didn't know how to tell him what was really going on. He would figure it out sooner or later, though.

Antwan had been working diligently with all B-Fresh's business ventures, along with his number of contacts in East Orange, New Jersey, and Inglewood. California had brought him a substantial amount of work, followed by an even more lucrative amount of income, which all meant less time to spend with Kim.

Kim however, didn't mind, actually, she enjoyed the free time. It gave her more time with the girls which was her new hobby.

After an intense rock-climbing challenge, Crystal, James, and Kim entered a small cave a few feet from the top of the mountain. They all began to unstrap their backpacks. Kim was the first to inflate her air mattress. Crystal gathered the box wine and plastic cups, while James started the fire.

Both women set on opposite sides of James. They sipped wine and ate cheese crackers. When they got to their second box of wine Crystal became talkative.

"So, James, what's going on with you and my girl?"

"What you mean?"

"Don't answer her, James. She's just being nosey," Kim expressed.

"I'm just saying, this is the third girls trip you've crashed. What's your angle? You looking to have some fun or a relationship? If it's just fun you're looking for, I want you to keep my mouth closed."

"Crystal why are you doing this?"

"Kim, you can't possibly expect me to let you have all of this fine piece of man to yourself." Crystal began rubbing her soft hands up and down James's thigh. He looked at Kim, wondering if it was okay. "Don't look at her. Kim, I know it's been some time since we've shared a man. What, senior year in college? I think Mr. James might be up to the challenge. You saw how his muscles were bulging out of that t-shirt while he climbed the mountain?" Crystal's hands now explored his arms, back, and chest. The whole time he looked at Kim.

The flickering from the light of the fire bounced off the wall of the cave. Kim looked nervous but quickly shook it off by downing her drink.

"Yes, it has been some time. I thought about having a threesome with Antwan, but I didn't want him judging me. Plus, he never asked."

"James, come on, pull out that dick of yours. Let us see what you're working with," ordered Crystal. Once again, he looked at Kim. She just shrugged her shoulders. "What you keep looking at her for? You don't like this?" Crystal peeled off her wife beater and sports bra. Her perky high yellow 36-D breasts and pink nipples rubbed against his arm. She grabbed both his hands and placed them on her breasts.

"Go ahead, touch 'em. My husband paid for them, but never play with 'em. Just like everything else he bought." Her hands began to unfasten his belt.

James squeezed and admired her breasts. Kim's eyes were fixated on what would escape his pants. She doubted if he was hung like Antwan. He was too cute to have a big dick.

"Umm, damn Mr. James. You holding out aren't you," spat Crystal. She stroked his nine-inch thick dick with both hands. James had a confident smirk on his face. He looked at Kim.

"Kim, this huge dick look like it tastes good. You want the first lick?"

"Nah, go ahead, you go first. Plus, it's not all that big."

James was caught off guard by her response. To his surprise, she looked a tad bit jealous. Crystal smacked his dick against her wet tongue. The scent of his sweaty balls and dove soap turned her on. She then sucked on the head of his dick. She licked the sides, catching her own saliva like ice cream dripping down the side of a cone. James kept eye contact with Kim, every time she looked down at Crystal giving him oral, he would make his dick jump, causing her to look back at him.

Crystal happened to open her eyes and look up. When she saw him looking at Kim and not watching her performance. She sidestepped his knee and positioned herself in between his legs. She removed his stiff cock from her mouth, then smacked his dick a few times to see how hard it was. Satisfied she allowed two big globs of spit to slide between her breasts as she held them together, she leaned forward and made James lie on his elbows. She then placed his long, thick dick in between her soft, round breasts. She squeezed them together and moved up and down jerking him off. Every time the head of his dick came up she used her skilled tongue to greet it.

"Oh, shit, damn lady! I never tittie fucked a woman with these kinds of skills.

"Huh, I got your full attention now?" Crystal boasted.

"Yeah, damn that shit feels good!" James moaned.

"Come on Kim, stop being shy. Put this dick in your mouth. It tastes good!" Crystal badgered Kim.

James watched as Kim lowered her head into his lap. The closer she got, the harder his dick became. Her soft sweet lips met the tip of his dick. First, she kissed it once and looked up at him. Then kissed it again, before slurping on the access cock that wasn't smothered in Crystal's cleavage. Her mouth was wet like he had stuck his dick into a glass of water. Her tongue twirled around the head of his dick, while her wet mouth devoured his shaft.

"Come on big, Daddy! It's time for you to fill this pussy up with that big dick of yours!" ordered Crystal.

Kim slurped on his dick a few more times and surprisingly came up and kissed Crystal. The way their lips and tongues danced together it was clear they'd had a lot of practice with each other before.

"I wanted to kiss you for three days now. What took you so long?" asked Crystal.

"People been around," answered Kim.

"Hold up! You two got some type of love affair going on?" Meanwhile, parading around like y'all best friends," James accused.

"Nah, after today us three will have a love affair. I'm tired of using a strap-on," explained Crystal.

She peeled off her jean shorts, revealing she wasn't wearing panties. She pushed James on his back and mounted him, butt ass naked with knee pads, elbow pads and Timberland boots. Her pussy was loose. It was wet but seemed a little too stretched out for James ten-inch piece. She felt his disconnect. The muscles in her pussy gripped his dick so tight he had to squeeze her ass to stop from busting. Crystal worked her hips slow, in small circles.

"Oww… yes! Yes, this dick feels good."

Kim decided to mount his face. As she squatted down, James peeked up at her runway strip and thought that the patch she had was the sexiest thing in the world. He licked his tongue to meet her clit. Chills crept up Kim's spine. His tongue was strong and pointy. He curled the tip to concentrate on her clit. James worked his hips and pelvis to the same rhythm of Crystal. She admired the gritty fuck face he forced out of Kim. There was no passion in the way Crystal rode his long dick. Each thrust, each grunt, each moan only had one destination. She was eager to cum and cum she did.

"Take this pussy. Yeah, umm…oh, oh, oh, yes, yes! Damn, you like this pussy, huh? That's my bitch's pussy you are tasting. It tastes good, don't it? Yeah, make us both cum. Yeah, make us both cummm…"

Kim lowered her pussy on his face. The juices from her cumming slid down on his chin. He lapped it up, wanting more. The two ladies engaged in a passionate kiss.

"Here your turn, ride this dick while I suck his balls and taste that sweet pussy of yours. I'm in the giving spirit, plus all my husband do is eat my pussy," ordered Crystal.

The fire caused all parties to sweat. The cave was already a little dark, but now the sunset from their location looked as if it was setting right across from them. Kim was the only one enjoying the view. She removed herself from his face and now was easing her way down the length of his dick.

James felt like a man who had just won the lottery. Kim's pussy was golden compared to Crystal's. The deeper he went the wetter she became. She rode him slow, taking her time to enjoy the view and his cock. Crystal was underneath, sucking each ball at a time. Her tongue would occasionally visit the crack of Kim's ass. When this happened, Kim would raise calling James's lips. He would kiss them until she pulled away.

"Umm…yeah, right there. That's it, James…right there!" Kim closed her eyes and sped up her rotation.

James could no longer hold back the urge to release his orgasm. Kim noticed his sudden hesitation. She hopped off his dick just in time.

"Uggh!" A large amount of cum splashed against Crystal's face. She laughed, then sucked his dick until each drop was down her throat.

Kim massaged his balls and planted soft kisses on his bare chest. The taste of his sweat and cologne turned her on.

"Damn, you two are going to drive me crazy. I can't believe Ant prefers them big two-hundred and fifty plus women over this. He has no idea."

"James what are you talking about?" asked Kim.

"And be careful, I still have your limp dick in my hands," warned Crystal.

"Nah, I'm just saying." He looked at the expression on Kim's face. She had no idea her husband had a BBW fetish. "I'm going to just keep my mouth closed. Looks like I already said too much."

"So, my husband told you out his own mouth he liked BBWs? Kim drilled him until he answered every question she had. He felt like a man under interrogation. Selfishly he thought, he was helping himself out until Crystal spoke.

"That's some real cruddy shit you doing? I mean, I know we all may be wrong for the sex, but you really sitting here snitching on your boy. I'm sorry, but I will never even look at that snitch dick of yours again. You just a foul ass nigga." Crystal gave him a disgusted look.

"Come on, Kim, let's go. And James don't worry, we'll make it back down this mountain without your help. You did enough for the day." Both women got dressed and suited up to leave.

James fixed his clothes and just stood there perplexed. He wanted to stop them, but he really wanted to stop Kim. She didn't even look at him. She just followed behind Crystal who knew the trail back down the mountain.

He shrugged his shoulders and said. "Fuck it, ain't like she could tell him, he told her."

CHAPTER NINE

Antwan sat in his home office doing what he loved best, crunching numbers and finding ways to get back as much money as he possibly could. Since it was tax season, he was having a hard time deciphering where seven hundred dollars went. Kim's credit card showed a medical co-payment for a doctor he'd never heard her speak about. He placed the thought in the back of his mind, piles of bills covered his desk. He began to organize the bills in each category. To his surprise, the name of the mysterious doctor appeared on a bill.

An uneasy feeling invaded Antwan's gut as he read the bill. His heart felt as if it weighed a ton. His head started to ache. The more he read the more it hurt. When he matched the dates to the events that occurred in their relationship the more he felt betrayed. Part of him was happy, he cheated on Kim. Without that edge, he had no idea how he would've handled this. He began to replay some of the words that came out her mouth.

"I want to have your baby. Let's start a family. You're my husband and we had an agreement to make a family one day."

"You, lying piece of shit." Antwan threw down the bill. He grabbed his jacket and headed for the door.

Kim stormed up the driveway bracing herself for a much-needed confrontation. She didn't even bother to retrieve her luggage. She fished around in her enormous LV bag for her keys when the door suddenly swung open. They were both startled for a moment.

"Just who I wanted to see," spat Antwan.

"Yeah, same here," Kim replied.

The couple partook in a stare down. Kim's was more of a display of anger. While Antwan's twitch of his lips exhibited nothing but disgust.

"Come in, no need for us to put on a show in front of our neighbors." Antwan moved aside for Kim to enter.

"So, you don't find me attractive? You had me get that surgery and you really like plus size women?"

"Look, I don't know what you talking about or who you got your information from. You trying to argue 'bout things you should already know. Of course, I like plus size women. I married one! You chose to get that surgery because it was something you wanted to do. More importantly, how could you get a procedure done for birth control, and not only keep it from me, but mislead me with all that talk about being ready to start a family?"

"What are you talking about?"

"Don't play stupid. I was doing the taxes and found out everything. You should of used a different address and paid your co-payment in cash."

"I wasn't ready to have a baby. You kept making a big deal about it. Crystal suggested I see her doctor. It's not permanent, I can go and get it removed whenever."

"So, Crystal runs our relationship? You'd rather take her advice and betray our marriage than talk to me? *Your husband!*"

"It's not like that, I swear! But, I don't see how or why you're upset. You don't want me anymore. When I lost the weight, I lost my husband. It's clear to me now, I messed up and you'll never forgive me for it."

"Don't try to do this. Don't switch this around in so many ways. Thinking if you take ownership, everything will be okay. You will not get your way. Not this time! I'm leaving for a couple days."

"What you mean you're leaving for a couple days? We're having a discussion that needs a resolution."

"Aren't you coming from a lil' vacation with your buddy, Crystal?"

"Yeah, and what does that have to do with this?"

"Maybe I need a vacation, too. Matter of fact, I'm going to call up James and see if he wants to go to Vegas or something for a few days. I need to think about how or what we're going to do. So, spending some time with my buddy won't be bad.

"Humph, your buddy. Please!"

"What does that mean?"

"Nothing! Go ahead and enjoy yourself. We both need to think this over." Kim walked away realizing she almost exposed her hand.

"Oh, you best believe, I'm going to enjoy myself. You can bet that!" Antwan walked to his car even more confused than before.

Why did she make that comment about James? Who told her all that information about him having a thing for plus size women? It didn't take Antwan long to figure things out.

"James!"

He navigated his Audi with one hand and reached for his cell phone, to call James. After a few tries, he gave up. This was no time for a voice message. He didn't want to alert him, so leaving a message would reveal his hand. He was too angry to suppress his frustration. Unconsciously, he drove his car not realizing where he was headed. He found himself pulling up in front of Hassana's Housing projects.

Hassana bolted from her well-cushioned stoop, not trying to allow Antwan a chance to see her in true project girl form, in her cut-off jean shorts, over top of a pair of leggings, a wife beater under her flannel shirt, and designer sneakers to match her designer head scarf.

"Girl, where you going? Fuck da police coming and you holding these niggas packs like we in high school again?" Argued her friend.

"No, that's my boss!" Hassana closed the door to her apartment.

Her friend looked up and watched Antwan's fine ass strut across the dirt field, where grass once was.

"How are you doing? Was that Hassana who just ran inside?"

"How you doing, Bossman? Yeah, that was her, she had to use the bathroom. She'll be right back in a few minutes."

"No problem, I'll cop a squat right here and wait." Deep in thought, Antwan began analyzing her living conditions. Did he have to give her another raise? Maybe she needed to stop spending all her money on designer clothes and save up to move.

Hassana threw on some jeans, red bottoms, a blouse and removed her scarf allowing her freshly hairdo to bounce when she pranced.

"Mr. Mitchell...I mean Antwan. What did I do to enjoy the pleasure of getting a home visit?"

"Come on, pack a bag. We going on a lil' vacation." Antwan said smiling.

Hassana eyed him strangely. "Huh, what are you talking about?"

74

"Gurl, you about to argue with his fine ass? You was just complaining about needing a trip." interrupted Janet.

"Janet, please." Hassana shrieked.

"Okay, okay, I'm out of here," Janet said, excusing herself.

"Look, I didn't mean to cause an issue. Don't even pack. We can do all the shopping you desire when we get there." Antwan continued.

"Gurl, you still standing there? Hurry up before he changes his mind." Janet yelled from the bottom of the porch.

"Janet!" Hassana screamed and rolled her eyes.

"Look, I know we have a lot to discuss. Since you been back to work, neither of us addressed our relationship. Let's go somewhere, anywhere you like. We can talk, shop and do whatever else your heart desires."

Hassana was literally turning to mush in his hands. He felt the perspiration build in the palm of her hand. Once he realized she became reluctant, Antwan snagged at her fingers. She didn't resist. Instead, she followed him to his car without speaking a word.

The Bahamas…

After spending one night in Miami shopping and dining. Antwan and Hassana hopped on a cruise to the Bahamas. Hassana wanted to go to Dubai, but since Antwan told her they only had three to four days, she settled for the Bahamas. Dubai would have needed at least six to eight days.

Both parties were a little restless. Not so much as tired in the need of sleep, they just needed to rest their minds and their bodies.

Chapter 1

Greed is a Bitch

Sadeek crept in the house at 4 a.m. trying not to wake Keisha. He lay on the couch and put one of his legs on the armrest. He had just begun to doze off when he was awakened by an ice-cold shower. "What the fuck?" Sadeek jumped up and tried to adjust his sight as water and ice cubes fell to the floor. "Yeah, muthafucka. You think you can just walk in my fucking house at four o'clock in the gotdamn morning and just lay your head down and go to sleep?" Keisha was pissed off. She was starting to hate even the thought of Sadeek.

"I was taking care of some shit. You lucky I ain't jump up and slap the shit out of you!" he yelled, walking to the kitchen and grabbing a few paper towels. Keisha was right on his heels, her black silk nighty and robe flying in the breeze.

"Yeah right, muthafucka! You ain't that crazy. But, you got to go," she yelled, slamming the empty cup on the counter.

"Go where? Why the fuck is you trippin' at four o'clock in the fucking mornin'?" He brushed past Keisha almost knocking her into the stove. She quickly caught her balance and followed him back into the living room.

"I don't give a fuck what time it is or where you go. I can make a suggestion though. Start with the bitch whose pussy you just climbed out of. Go back and knock on her fucking door!" Kiesha stood in the middle of the room with hands on her hips. Lips twisted, eyes squinted and breathing heavy.

"I wasn't with no bitch. I was taking care of business." Sadeek's voice got louder. He fidgeted with his ring, avoiding eye contact as was his habit when he was lying his ass off.

"Look, I can't take this shit no more. You got to get the fuck out. You can leave by will or by force; you draw it up," Keisha persisted.

Sadeek glanced at Keisha and bit his bottom lip while rubbing his hands together as he tried to calm down. He wanted to knock the shit out of her. His fists were balled up, but he wasn't crazy. He knew Malik would take his fucking head. More reason for him to hurry up and get rid of this nigga.

"Step lively, muthafucka. And give me my keys." Keisha held her hand out with major attitude.

Sadeek reluctantly handed her the keys and headed to the door. "I guess you can go back to playing house with Malik."

"Don't worry about what the fuck I do with Malik. You just worry about those dirty bitches you stick your dick in."

Sadeek paused then responded, "If you weren't so busy giving my pussy to the next nigga, I wouldn't be fucking other bitches." He gave Keisha a dirty look and headed out the door, he figured he'd hit his boy Tone's house.

Keisha shut the door behind him. Sheeit . . . you damn right I'm fucking Malik and his dick is good as hell. He was all up in it the other day. She wiped up the remaining water off the floor. Headed to her bedroom and hopped in bed. As she drifted off, she mumbled, "Fuck that nigga!"

Later that day . . .

Sadeek walked in the Peppermint Lounge razor sharp, sporting a pair of crisp dark colored jeans laying on top of his grey Timberland boots, a charcoal grey sweater, and a lightweight dark blue three-quarter leather jacket. His short fade and freshly shaped mustache and goatee enhanced his smooth brown caramel skin. In Sadeek's world, nobody could tell him shit. As he made his way to the back where Raheem was sitting, niggas were shouting him out while bitches were checking him out. He nodded, shook a few hands, and grabbed a shot of Grey Goose while passing the bar and kept on moving. When he reached Raheem's table, he could see him dismissing this fine, brown-skinned honey. She saw Sadeek coming and rolled her eyes as she slid out the booth.

"Don't be salty, shorty," Sadeek said with a smile. The young woman just kept on going.

"What's up superstar nigga?" Raheem said as he extended his hand to Sadeek.

"Sheeit. I can't call it. It's your world squirrel; I'm just trying to bust a nut," he said, slapping hands with Raheem. They both busted out laughing as Sadeek slid into the booth. Raheem flagged down the waitress and ordered them some drinks.

Sadeek and Raheem downed their drinks and laughed about Keisha throwing ice-cold water on him in the middle of the night. Retelling the story caused Sadeek's whole mood to change.

"I hate that bitch sometimes," he spat as he guzzled down his shot of Hennessy then chased it down with a double deuce Heineken.

"What the fuck are you talking about 'Deek?" Raheem said in a drunken slur.

"Fuckin' Keisha!" Sadeek said with a hateful tone. "Man get the fuck outta here. You know good and well you love that girl. That's why your ass sitting up here pouting like a fuckin' bitch."

"Fuck you, Rah. She done put me out for the last fucking time."

"That's what you said last time. This ain't the fucking Oprah sofa, nigga. You, betta handle that shit," Raheem said then started laughing.

"On the real, Rah, I think it's time to make that move."

"What you talking about?" Raheem asked.

"The way I see it, we been working for that nigga for over ten years and we still make just as much as the new jacks. He charges us like he don't know us. Shit, the way I figure, we cut out the middleman and we could be making all the money. Just take over this whole fucking city."

"Nigga, you trippin'."

"Shit, I ain't trippin'. What? You scared mu'fucka?"
"Scared? Hell no, I ain't scared of nothing or no one."

Raheem said giving Sadeek a look that said don't you ever question my manhood.

"A'ight then. You ready for a fucking war?"

"Hell yeah. At any moment, but for something worth warring over. In that case, I ain't got no problem with war. I just ain't trying to go to war over no gotdamn pussy. Especially, if it ain't pussy that belongs to me."

"This shit is way past pussy. It's about principle. That nigga know he fucking owe us. And we ain't sitting on the side waiting no fucking more. We getting ready to take it. You down or what?"

The next thing that comes out his mouth better be right or he's going on the list with Malik. Sadeek thought as he stared at Raheem.

Raheem stared in space for a minute then took a pull on his blunt.

"Yeah, I'm down. But make sure it's for principle and not for greed. Because greed is a bitch," he said.

Raheem thought he and Sadeek had done some cruddy shit but was he ready to help him take Malik out? Shit, for the last couple of weeks he was trying to come up with a plan to get the fuck out. Now, this nigga was talking about going to war and taking over. This was some shit he would have to talk over with his main man, Nine.

After his talk with Raheem, Sadeek put his plan in motion, which would call for a trip to Detroit. That was how he was going to get his come up and his revenge.

****

Keisha was walking through Short Hills Mall with her aunt Pat bringing her up to speed on the other night when she had to check Sadeek's ass. Pat was only ten years older than her and had raised her due to her mom dealing with an addiction.

"Hell, yeah I threw that shit on that nigga and told him to get the fuck out," Keisha bragged.

"Bitch, you lucky he ain't slap your ass down," Pat joked.

"I'll tell you like I told him, he ain't that crazy," Keisha said as they dipped into Saks Fifth Avenue and headed right for the makeup counter.

"So how many days are you going to let pass before you let him back this time?" Aunt Pat asked. She leaned into the mirror trying on some mascara.

"Fuck him. I'm done. I hate to see that nigga coming; his very touch makes my fucking skin crawl," Keisha said with apparent anger in her voice.

"Yeah right, bitch. You say that shit all the time then that nigga be right back in there." Pat took the time to point out.

"Don't judge me. I got to do what I got to do. The only reason I still fucks with that nigga Sadeek is because it's good for business." Keisha applied blush to her cheeks.

"How is fucking, Sadeek's boss good for business? That shit is dangerous."

Keisha stopped dead in her tracks and looked at her aunt. "Look, I don't get in your business, so do both of us a favor and don't get in mine." Keisha started to walk away, but Pat grabbed her by the arm.

"Hold up, Key. Look, I love you. That's the only reason why I'm saying something."

Keisha stopped but didn't turn around. She took a deep breath and thought about her aunt's words. "I know. I'm caught up, Auntie." She paused. "I'm in love with a man I can't have. And I hate the one that I'm with." A tear ran down her face. She turned and grabbed a tissue from the counter and patted her cheek.

"Regardless of what I say, I know that Malik loves you and he got your back. Just be careful, Key. Sadeek ain't stupid . . . and he's crazy. That is a dangerous cocktail. I

84

don't want anything to happen to you," Pat said as she hugged her niece.

"Thanks, Auntie. I'm working on it." She hugged her back.

"A'ight bitch, let's go 'cause I got to put a dent in this nigga's bankroll. Fuck what you heard, this is going to be the most expensive piece of pussy that nigga ever had," Pat said, trying to lighten the mood as she let go of Keisha.

"You so crazy." Keisha laughed. As they headed to the designer purses, her Aunt Pat's words rang out in her head "be careful." Keisha had been feeling the danger of messing with both Sadeek and Malik for the past week and praying that all the shit she had been doing didn't blow up in her face.

CHRONICLES OF A BBW

Chapter 2

Making a Deal

Sadeek walked out the airport with his carry-on bag, looked around, jumped on a shuttle bus and headed to Enterprise. Within twenty minutes, he arrived at the Days Inn motel at the Metro airport in Detroit; he figured he could kill two birds with one stone by making this trip for both business and pleasure, so he arranged to have Kim already there when he arrived. Kim, a bitch he'd met the last time he and Malik were there was already waiting for him in his room. Since his meeting was set for 8 P.M. with the headman, who was Malik's connect, Sadeek figured until then, he could get his dick sucked and lay in some warm pussy. A few minutes after he walked into his room, Kim was riding the hell out of him. Once he busted his first nut, he turned over onto his stomach and prepared to doze off. "In an hour, order something to eat and then wake me up," Sadeek told Kim.

"No problem. Shit, you hooked me up. I'll just return the favor." She smiled. Turning on the television, she flicked the channels until she found something to watch and eventually dozed off.

By seven P.M. Sadeek had eaten the Chinese food Kim had ordered and put on his clothes, boots, and jewels. He looked in the mirror and then walked over to Kim. "Are you going to be here when I get back?"

"Hell yeah. I need to get thanked for that meal." She flashed a pretty smile.

Kim was definitely a dime. At 5'6", 130 pounds, legs thick, and a shapely small waist accented with a flat toned stomach. Her 36C breasts looked ever so suckable. Her toned arms led to small manicured hands that just a few hours ago were wrapped nicely around Sadeek's dick. She wore her shoulder length hair in a bun with a Chinese bang, accenting her pretty pear diamond shaped eyes that seemed to glisten with every blink. And oh yes, that smile.

Sadeek smiled, grabbed her by the waist, and kissed her lips. He patted her on the butt. "I'll see you later," he said then headed out the door.

It was a forty-five-minute drive to Dread's estate. When he got there, he was greeted by Scarie, the go between guy. Scarie set up all the meetings with the connects and that included more than fifteen states and two overseas spots. Of course, he was running the weed distribution in Jamaica. Dread had shit on lock and with the help of Sadeek's greed; Scarie was getting ready to loosen some of Dread's grip. Sadeek had only met both of them in person one time but had been gaining notice by Scarie because of his heart and fearlessness, along with the rumor of his dissatisfaction with Malik. It would be just what he needed to set a plan of his own in action.

Sadeek pulled up to the gate and he could not believe his eyes. The house looked like the fucking president lived there. Big willow trees and manicured lawns with ground keepers scurrying around to keep shit in order. The house had a modern castle look to it.

Scarie waved him through the gate then it slammed closed behind him. He followed him to the house then was appointed a parking spot. Sadeek parked, got out, and shook hands with his soon to be partner. They stood trying to have a conversation when three Cadillac golf carts drove toward them. One was driven by Dread, and the other two by his bodyguards carrying AK47s. Dread was an older Jamaican dude who grew up in London then settled in Toronto, Canada. Lots of those Jamaican cats would come and run shit in Detroit. Dread stepped out of the cart and looked Sadeek up and down like: What the fuck is he doing here? He walked right past him and his bodyguards followed suit.

Sadeek looked at Scarie then whispered, "What's up with that?"

"Don't worry, it's all good. Did you bring the money?" Scarie tried to comfort him.

"Yeah. It's all here," Sadeek said, still leery of the interaction he had just had with the top man.

"Come on," Scarie said, walking toward the steps.

Sadeek reluctantly followed.

They entered the house and the shiny floors and huge statues of half and fully naked women amazed Sadeek. Exotic plants and paintings adorned the wall. They walked down a long hallway and entered an office on the first floor. Dread was seated comfortably behind his huge mahogany desk. He reached inside a small wooden box, took a fat spliff, and lit it up. Then he inhaled and blew a big cloud of smoke toward Sadeek. Scarie whispered in Dread's ear. Dread broke the silence with his thick Jamaican accent.

"What the fuck you come by me, pussy boi. Me nah know you?" The statement threw Sadeek totally off.

Sadeek squinted, and his eyebrows wrinkled. "I met you one time. I came to Detroit with Malik before," Sadeek managed to get out in a low voice.

"What's dat you carry der, boi?"

"It's the money I am offering you to start our new business venture." Small beads of sweat formed on Sadeek's brow. Dread looked as if his next move was going to be giving the order to rob and kill this nigga. One eyebrow was raised and the other rested over a squinted eye.

"You got balls bona coming wit' dis amount of money. You trying to bring trouble 'pon me?"

"Nah. I'm just ready to come up. I figure I can help you and you can help me," Sadeek said, obviously getting upset at how the whole thing was going down. He bit his bottom lip and tapped the side of his leg.

"You have no seniority to come here. Take this bumbaras from fronta me!" Dread slammed his hand on the desk, staring Sadeek dead in his eyes.

"Look Dread, I'm hungry. I'm ready to take this shit to the next level!" Sadeek made one last plea.

"How you gon' come to me house speakin' all freestyle? Me nah know you, pussy clot. Get the fuck outta here for me dead you!" With that statement, Dread's bodyguards moved toward him.

Sadeek backed up. Scarie quickly grabbed Sadeek by the arm. "I'll see him out."

When they got to the car, he said to Sadeek, "Look, go to the hotel. I will be there in about an hour."

"What the fuck is going on? I thought you said he would be ready to do business?" Sadeek asked.

"Look, go to the room. It's a change of plans. I'll talk to you when I get there," Scarie reassured him.

Sadeek turned his head, looking down and rubbing his hands together. He looked up at Scarie as his nostrils flared. No, the fuck you didn't get me all the way out here for this shit.

Scarie picked right up on the thought and said, "Trust me. Let me defuse this shit and I'll meet you in an hour."

Sadeek jumped in his ride and headed back to the hotel. Who the fuck do that Dread nigga think he fucking with? Yeah, I got his pussy clot all right.

When Scarie returned to Dread's office, all he got was dirty looks. "What the fuck, boi? You getting weak? Must be all that coke you put up your nose," Dread growled.

With hatred in his eyes, Scarie glared at him. "He is Malik's boi. He is just trying to do a little something on the side, so I thought . . ."

Dread cut him off. "You thought. You thought what? That I would want a stranger standing in mi fuckin' house. Oh, then you thought that I would do business with a nigga mi don't know? The main ting I have always taught you, boi, is loyalty. Mi about loyalty. Mi a deal with Malik. Mi don't know that other muthafucka. Don't bring him near me again. Him have a look of a vampire, and him won't quench his thirst here."

Dread sucked his teeth. "You're dismissed."

Scarie left the office feeling like a five-year-old. But he would be feeling like a grown ass man by the end of the night.

Back at the hotel...

Sadeek pulled into the hotel parking lot still mad as hell. He had a taste for blood and didn't give a fuck whose blood it was. When he got to the room, he was greeted by the lovely he had left there, butt-naked and horny. As soon as he closed the door, she went to her knees, pulled out his dick and looked at him with a sneaky grin.

"I was waiting for him." She said referring to his dick. "Damn shorty, you going to make me take you   home
with me," he said, rubbing the top of her head.
Stopping to get a handful of hair to hold his balance.

"Don't talk, just listen," she said, taking him into her mouth. Kim began licking and sucking all over the head and then forced him to the back of her throat. Slurping and slobbing all over his dick. Sadeek's knees buckled.

"Oh shit . . . hold up, baby . . ."

"Mmmmm . . ." She continued to bring on his intense orgasm. After ten more minutes, all she heard was "Aaaahhhh. . . Oh my god!"

He pulled her hair tighter and released in her mouth. She sucked him until the last drop was gone. Easing him out her mouth, she ran her tongue down his shaft and sucked lightly on his balls. Electrical shocks shot up and down his spine.

"Shit . . . you trying to fuck with a nigga's emotions."

As she rose to her feet, she gave him a look that said it all. Walking over to the dresser, she took a shot of gin and lit a blunt. Sadeek fell back on the bed in an attempt to pull himself together, then took off his pants and boxers. Turning around to see he was still at attention excited her. She walked over to the bed while taking long drags on the blunt.

"He needs you to—"

"No problem." She climbed on top of him and eased down slowly on his dick, giving him the ride of a lifetime. Forty-five minutes later, he was laid the fuck out.

His cell rang and Sadeek answered, "Hello."

"I'll be there in about fifteen minutes," Scarie said, his strong accent came blaring through the phone.

"A'ight," he said then disconnected the call.

Sadeek headed to the shower. "I got somebody coming by here in about fifteen minutes. Can you straighten up for me?" he asked.

"I got you, baby," Kim replied.

When he came out, Kim had straightened up and dipped off, so he called her phone. "What's up? Why you dip?"

"I'll be back in an hour. I need to get some clothes."
"Okay, I'll see you later."

Just then, he heard a knock at the door and went to open it. "What's up, my dude?" Sadeek said, shaking Scarie's hand. Scarie came in and sat at the table.

"Can I light up one of these blunts?" Scarie needed to get his head tight for what he was getting ready to say. Once he lit up, he took a deep breath and began his proposition.

"You kill my boss. I'll kill yours."

Sadeek seized the blunt from Scarie, took a big hit, and immediately began to cough. Sixty seconds passed as he sat there staring at him processing the information. "Let's do it," Sadeek finally said.

Scarie began rubbing his hands together. "Dread has one love—the strip club. He goes every Thursday night, which is a day away, so we have to move on this shit." Scarie was running the plan as if he had had it down for months. Sadeek just sat there taking it all in and nodding his head.

"Dread always gets a private lap dance, some head, and maybe even some pussy depending on the mood. I'm planning to put him in the room with the hidden door, that way you can slip in and out undetected. The bodyguards will be posted outside the door unaware of the execution-taking place on the other side. Club 4 Play has some of the baddest bitches in attendance, so a distraction is not impossible but, be quick and have as less a struggle as possible." When Scarie finished laying the framework for his plan, he shook hands with Sadeek and headed to the door. He turned and said, "Meet me at the downtown spot at nine o'clock p.m. Don't be late." Then he was gone just as quick as he came.

After Scarie left, Sadeek drank half a bottle of gin trying to wrap his head around the fact that he had come out here to make a deal with the headman and ended up in cahoots with the man's very partner. What the fuck had the universe just put in his lap? Just when he got ready to second-guess the situation, he heard a knock at the door. He checked the peephole before opening it. Kim stood there in a Versace black strapless body dress and a pair of stilettos.

"Hey, Mr. Sexy. Did you miss me?" she asked once he let her inside.

"Hell yeah, but I think he missed you more." He grabbed his dick and began stroking it. She smiled, already well aware of what he was capable of doing with it. For the rest of the night, they sucked and fucked each other into a stupor. Sadeek forgot all about what lay ahead; he was in heaven and didn't want to leave.

****

Thursday night came, and everything went just as planned. Scarie put a girl on Dread that he knew he could not resist, and as usual, he went in the room all alone. She danced sensually, grinding on him as Sadeek waited in the cut. As soon as the woman pulled Dread's dick out and started to suck, he lay back on the large couch and closed his eyes. While Sadeek was squatting down waiting for his attack, sweat was running down his back and face as he tried to control his breathing. He began to slide along the wall getting closer to the trap door. He reached out, cracked it, and saw Dreads contorted face as the woman worked his steel.

Sadeek took a deep breath, jumped out from the side of him, and cut Dread's throat from ear to ear. The woman fell back with fear in her eyes as blood ran from Sadeek's blade. Dread struggled for a few seconds then lumped over to the side. Sadeek grabbed the woman by the arm and forced her into the small opening, then he climbed in right behind her. Just like that, he and the woman smoothed out the secret door without a trace.

When they got to the alley, Sadeek's adrenalin was working overtime. He ran one way and the girl ran the other. He looked back and saw her being snatched into a black van. Sadeek turned and kept running until he neared the block where he was to be picked up. The headlights of a vehicle flashed twice, and he sprinted to the vehicle. The door popped open and he dove in. All he heard was the doors lock and tires screech. He lay on his back, head up against the door and breathing heavy. Once they arrived a few blocks from the motel, he jumped out, pulled his hat down, and then shoved his hands in his hoodie pocket. Looking in all directions, Sadeek began double-timing his pace.

Back at the motel room, Sadeek was all charged up, looking at the blood staining his hands and shoes. He walked in the room.

"What the fuck happened to you?" Kim ran over to him.

"Nothing. Watch out." He pushed past her and went to the bathroom. Clearly, she was not trying to hear that.

"Are you okay? Let me help you." She knocked on the bathroom door.

The door flew open. Sadeek stormed out and pushed her back toward the wall.

"Didn't I fucking tell you to get the fuck back? Don't make me slap the shit out of you."

She looked at him like an arm was growing out of his head. Her eyes narrowed, and her breathing increased. She balled up her fist tight. As he turned to walk away, Kim tapped him on the shoulder. He turned, and she punched him dead in the nose. He fell back on the bed as she followed up with three more blows, cursing and yelling in now what sounded like a Jamaican accent.

"You don't know who you mess wit', boi."

Sadeek managed to get her off him and the tables had quickly turned; he was now choking the shit out of her. He blacked out for about forty seconds and when he came to he had choked the very life out of her.

"Oh shit . . . what the fuck?" he said, jumping up and walking around the room holding his hands up to his head. "What the fuck did I just do? Shit! I got to get the fuck out of here." Grabbing everything that could link him to the room, he wiped shit down as Kim's lifeless body lay on the edge of the bed. Picking her up, he placed her in the middle of the bed. Her body is still so warm, he thought as he looked her over. Her breasts sat up firm and perky. He slid his hand between her legs and felt her moistness. "Shit, I was planning on getting some more of this. Why didn't you just shut the fuck up like I told you?" With that thought, he put on a condom, got on top of her, and pumped until he came. Snatching off the condom, he put it in a napkin on the edge of the nightstand and then pulled up his pants. Careful to leave no evidence behind, he put the napkin in his pocket, grabbed his stuff and rolled out.

When he was good and on his way home, he called Scarie to let him know he was leaving town. He drove back to Jersey with haunting thoughts of killing Dread and the girl. Then came the demented thought of how good she felt even after she was dead.

Sadeek arrived in Newark the next afternoon and checked into the Robert Treat Hotel downtown. Then he placed a call to Raheem and asked him to meet him there.

When they met up, Sadeek revealed everything except that he'd killed a woman and then fucked her corpse. Sadeek then laid out the plan to kill Malik and informed him that it was already in progress.

Raheem was starting to feel uneasy. He walked over to the window and stared at the New York skyline, tossing the information around in his head for a few minutes. Walking over to the table he sat in silence, and for the first time, he had absolutely nothing to say. Raheem watched Sadeek stare off into space with coldness to his eyes. He could see that Sadeek had gone to the extreme and there was no coming back. Raheem didn't have a problem with a come up, but to the demise of Malik, was it worth it?

Even though Malik was charging them a grip, they were making a grip and he had never disrespected them. In fact, it was the total opposite. That nigga would give you the shirt off his back then ask you if you needed his pants. Raheem looked at Sadeek with a blank expression. It was like he didn't know him. The stench of greed and pride oozed from his pores; his very soul was on fire. And

Raheem couldn't just see it; it was more like he smelled it and he knew the scent of death would follow. He decided to just go along for now until he could figure out the next move.

Chapter 3

The Twins

What's up, my nigga?" Sadeek said to Tah'leek letting himself into his apartment.

"Ain't nothing, nigga," Tah'leek said, leaning

up from the couch to shake hands with his twin brother. Since birth the two were inseparable. Only a few could tell them apart only added to their closeness. However, lately Tah'leek was having a huge disconnect with his brother. Tah'leek was ready to leave the streets while his twin was diving head first into very deep and dangerous waters.

Sadeek sat on the love seat across from his brothe and wasted no time giving him the update on their next move. "So, everything is in motion. I went to Detroit and met with the headman. He will be here in about a week to meet with all of us. I want you to be my right hand."

Tah'leek processed the information.

"So, what about Malik?"

"He's a dead man and don't even know it," Sadeek answered real smooth like it was nothing. Tah'leek sat up, grabbed the bottle of Jack and took it to the head. Sadeek watched his brother kill the liquor and not respond as if he wasn't down.

"So, what the fuck? You ain't ready for this change of hands." Sadeek looked disappointed.

"This ain't no change of hands. Your ass went out there and got in bed with some fucking strangers. How the fuck you know these muthafucka's are going to honor their word? You went out there, killed their boss, and then they gave you some see-thru ass promise. What guarantee do you have?"

"What the fuck are you talking about?" Sadeek rose from his seat "You act like you ain't trying to have my back."

Tah'leek stood. "Muthafucka, I have had your back from day one. Your greed got you making dumb ass moves."

"Man, fuck this. I'm giving you, my blood, an opportunity to be at the head of the table with me and you acting like I done signed our souls over to the devil," he yelled.

"That's what the fuck I'm talking about. It's all about you wanting something. Every time you want something my shit gets fucked up."

Sadeek stood eye to eye with his twin brother. It was like looking at his own face, but instead of seeing happiness, all he saw was disappointment. He stepped back nodding his head up and down.

"You know what? You right. It is about what I want. And I'm going to kill anybody that stands in the way of that."

"You threatening me, 'Deek?" Tah'leek asked with a bit of pain in his voice.

"Nah playboy. No threat necessary. The shit has been put on the table, you draw up." Sadeek, for the first time, turned his back on his brother. Headed to the door with hate in his heart and power on his mind, he didn't give a fuck who he would have to step on to get it.

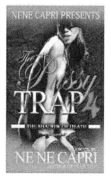

NENE CAPRI PRESENTS

Available in Paperback..!!

The Pussy Trap series 1 -5
Trust No Bitch series 1-3
Tainted 1 & 2
Diamonds Pumps & Glocks
Late Night Lick Vol. 1, 5, 6, 8, 10, 11
By NeNe Capri

Chastity Adams Presents

Gangsta Lovin' 1 & 2
Love Sex & Mayhem 1 & 2
Treacherous Desire
Late Night Lick Vol. 2, 4, 7 & 9
Unsacred Matrimony
By Chastity Adams

We Ship to Prisons:
Po Box 741581
Riverdale, GA 30274

N. TROUBLE

Made in the USA
Monee, IL
26 July 2021

74060317R00062